WITCHES
OF THE
WOOD

EDITED BY AIMEE RENEE

BIG SMALL TOWN BOOKS

BIG SMALL TOWN BOOKS

Published by Big Small Town Books
WWW.BIGSMALLTOWNBOOKS.COM

Big Small Town Books is a registered trademark, and the Big Small Town Books colophon is a trademark of Big Small Town Entertainment.

Big Small Town Books supports copyright. Thank you for purchasing an authorized edition of this book and for following copyright laws by not copying, scanning, or distributing any part of this work in any form without permission from the publisher. Formal requests may be sent to:

Big Small Town Books
P.O. Box 311
Unicoi, Tennessee, 37692

Reviewers may quote brief passage as part of their reviews.

This book may be ordered in bulk quantities for educational or promotional purposes. Please contact the publisher directly to inquire about discounted bulk ordering.

Paperback ISBN 978-1-7341660-0-2 • Also available as an eBook.

Printed in the United States of America. This book is set in 11-point Baskerville typeface.

10 9 8 7 6 5 4 3 2 1   19 20 21 22 23 24 25

LIBRARY OF CONGRESS CATALOGING-IN-PUBLICATION DATA IS AVAILABLE.

"The forest did not tolerate frailty of body or mind. Show your weakness and it would consume you without hesitation."

—*Tahir Shah*

CONTENTS

CONTENTS (CONT)

WITCHES
OF THE
WOOD

LEGACY

BEKAH HARRIS

Through a screen of thick fog and headlights, the house appeared like an apparition from another time. Abby squinted against the pouring rain as her new home rose up at the end of the gravel drive and loomed over the car. Dozens of windows illuminated by soft light stared back at them as her father pulled around to the back door and cut the engine.

Centuries-old oaks and maples stretched to the sky, their branches reaching out as if begging for mercy and casting eerie shadows against brick and glass.

Abby shivered, despite the mid-July heat. The fine hairs

of her arms rose on end, her skin tingling as if she had touched a live current.

Dad squeezed her hand.

"It won't be so creepy in the daylight," he promised.

Abby had grown up with stories about this place, usually told on windy nights as Halloween approached. Supposedly, the mansion was cursed by a dark history of lost love, slavery, and suicide. And her parents had never taken her to visit—not even once.

She'd never even met Great Aunt Jessie, a stern, reclusive "spinster" who had "unhealthy" interests in taxidermy and the occult, or so Abby had been told.

But eccentric family members and old, creaky mansions were the perfect formula for ghost stories. Reality was always less exciting when examined in the sunlight, away from rain, darkness, and shadows. Besides, her aunt Jessie had been 102 years old when she had died, and she'd made it that long without going nuts or falling victim to some supernatural curse.

The psycho genes came from Abby's mom's side of the family anyway.

Still, the creep factor of this place was off the charts. Dad was right. The night was playing tricks on her mind.

"Things will look better in the morning," Dad assured her. "I spent almost every summer out here when I was a kid. Come on, you're going to love it." He paused, grasping the door handle and flashed a mischievous grin. "Wait…you're not *chicken*, are you?"

"Um, *no*," Abby tried to ignore the swaying branches

and moving shadows, but her heart picked up speed.

"Okay, just making sure. I thought you were *tougher* than that."

He held her eyes for a moment and then opened the car door and dashed through the rain, his feet sending splatters of puddled rainwater in his wake.

Abby groaned and opened the door, pulling the hood of her rain jacket over her head. She grabbed her overnight duffel from the backseat and trotted head-down against the rain after her dad. He unlocked the door, which creaked open and swallowed them as they stepped inside the dimly-lit kitchen.

"Well, what do you think?" Dad asked. "Not exactly your mom's bungalow in Danville, is it?"

Or her sterile room at the behavioral clinic.

Dad's question reopened old wounds. The words flew from her mouth before she could stop them.

"Do we have to bring Mom into *everything?*" Abby snapped. "*You* left *her*, remember? *We* left her. And she told us to go and never look back. I wish you'd take her advice."

Dad stared down at his feet and clenched his fists. "I'm doing it again," he said. "I'm sorry."

In only seconds, Abby had torn away the fragile walls of her father's optimism, revealing what little remained of who he was since his wife had gone totally batshit. Sometimes, Abby forgot how much damage a few words could do, how much pain he concealed for her benefit.

"Hey, no worries," Abby said. She cleared her throat.

"Like you said, it's time for a fresh start."

Abby fabricated a smile and swallowed the guilt that had risen in her throat before it could choke her.

After her mom's third suicide attempt, she'd checked herself into the Lifebridge Mental Health Facility and told them to stop visiting. Not even a month later, her mom's attorney had sent Dad the divorce papers. That was more than a year ago, and Abby was still trying to process how much their lives had spiraled ever since. Looking at her father now was like seeing a ghost.

So when her ancient Aunt Jessie had kicked the proverbial bucket and left her entire estate to Abby and her father, Dad had convinced her to leave the blue grass of Kentucky to start a new life in the hills of Tennessee. He had promised this would be the beginning of better things. So far, the move had only managed to frizz out her hair and give her the creeps.

"So is there a place for us to sleep tonight?" Abby asked.

Dad shrugged. "The caretaker was supposed to change all the sheets and clean yesterday, so you should have your pick of any of the rooms you want. Did I tell you there are *three* floors and a *basement*?"

"Only about a thousand times," Abby said.

She hefted her duffel over her shoulder and followed Dad through the kitchen and hallway that connected to a cavernous great room. Abby gaped at the gleaming hardwood floors, floral wallpaper, and portraits of dead family members that hung in silent judgment on the walls.

A grand fireplace drew her eye beyond an impressive collection of antique furniture to the far wall, where a massive painting of Aunt Jessie was mounted above the mantel.

Growing up, she had heard plenty of stories about her great aunt, but she'd never seen pictures. Aunt Jessie's wiry figure stood straight as an iron post, her long bony fingers resting atop an ornate wooden cane she obviously didn't need for support. She was clad in Victorian garb, her white hair swept up in a tight bun that hadn't been in fashion for, like, a century.

Eccentric, Abby reminded herself.

"I thought you said Aunt Jessie didn't like to be photographed," Abby said.

"She didn't." Her dad hurried across the room, dodging end tables and flower arrangements, gesturing toward the portrait. "But she went all out for this. Look at that!"

"Oh, I see it," Abby said.

Her dad looked back at her, his eyes bright with excitement. "She always said she wanted to commission a portrait before she died. I guess she finally did."

He stepped back and admired the artist's rendering. "It's *amazing*," he said. "Come look at the detail. You can see the brushstrokes."

Abby stayed where she was, fighting off a chill as she met Aunt Jessie's sharp green eyes, which stared back at her, hawk-like and fierce, as if daring her to approach. It was quite possibly the most disturbing thing Abby had ever seen, but she kept her mouth shut, as her dad rambled on about Aunt Jessie's disdain for all things modern.

Abby forced her attention away from the painting, her eyes darting from the grand chandelier that hung from the vaulted ceiling to the double staircases that curved upward from the marbled entryway to the floor above.

Her dad shuffled away from Aunt Jessie, leaving her to preside over the dim room like a disapproving church matron. He hustled beside Abby, whistling when he took in the grand entryway.

"This was your mother's favorite part of the house," Dad said. "The last time we were here visiting, she asked if it would be too juvenile to slide down the banisters. And she did. Just like a little girl. We laughed and laughed until we realized Aunt Jessie was watching, had seen the whole thing. I don't think *she* thought it was too funny. But it was the last time I heard your mom laugh—*really* laugh—you know, that deep belly laugh she had when she was having fun…"

Abby bit her tongue until she tasted blood and fought back the memories.

She'd forgotten that Mom and Dad had spent the weekend here before their lives had gone to hell. Two days after they came home, Mom had suffered a grand mal seizure and promptly lost her mind.

Dad cleared his throat and hurried away from the staircase, as if stepping foot on the marble would be too painful. Instead, he turned abruptly and hurried from the room, leading Abby back the way they'd come.

"I've always loved this place," he said. "I can't believe it's mine. *Ours.* We're going to be happy here, Abs. Just you wait."

Abby smiled and followed her dad to a different part of the house, clenching her jaw as they traveled through dark, passage-like hallways, stopping in front of a steep, narrow set of stairs.

"Back in its heyday, the servants would use these." Her father yawned. "I'm beat. Let's find a place to crash."

The back stairs to the second level screeched like scared cats as Abby climbed them, and she could feel a persistent draft all around her, which grew stronger the higher she climbed. Goosebumps pebbled her arms.

Old houses are drafty, she told herself.

But she couldn't fight the sensation that there was someone behind her. Someone breathing down the back of her neck.

Aunt Jessie's creepy portrait flashed in her memory.

Abby whirled around on the stairs, wobbling dangerously until she steadied herself on the rail. Taking a deep breath, she studied the empty space. No one was behind her; nothing was there.

Which made perfect sense considering she and Dad were the only people in the house. *Weren't they?*

"Abby, you coming?"

"Yeah, Dad," she called. "So is there anyone else staying here? You mentioned a caretaker and servants' stairs."

"Just us," he said. His voice echoed from somewhere in the hallway at the top of the stairs. "The caretaker lives across the river, and the house hasn't been staffed since before I was born."

Abby took one last look down the empty stairwell and then hurried to catch up with him. The hallways were covered in ornate wallpaper that sprouted up from the wainscoting in blossoms and ivy. Gleaming hardwood reflected the overhead light on either side of a Turkish rug that ran the length of the floor. Abby felt like she had been transported back in time to a place she didn't belong. But her father? He stopped at every door, detailing memories and telling stories.

Finally, he rounded the corner and stopped at the end of the hall, pushing open a wide wooden door, its surface carved with an intricate pattern of leaves and vines.

"I've wanted to stay in the master bedroom since I was barely big enough to climb the stairs," he said. "I only got to sleep in here once. Aunt Jessie only allowed it because I was her favorite nephew. And now, she's left this whole place—"

Dad trailed off as he scanned the room, taking in every detail.

"You know, I used to be terrified of this room when I was a kid. Seems silly now that I'm moving in."

It didn't seem silly to Abby at all.

The room was like an animal graveyard, horrifying to her sixteen-year-old sensibilities. She couldn't imagine having to stand in the room for five minutes as a seven-year-old. Dead creatures of all varieties stood erect and life-like, mounted on stands and posed mid-action, as if they could spring to life at any moment.

A red fox stared at her from atop a tall chest of drawers. Its yellow eyes focused on some unseen spot in the distance, its sharp white teeth bared in an open mouth. A raccoon sat back on its haunches behind the fox, holding its paws to its mouth as if eating. They were everywhere: cats, dogs, squirrels, woodchucks, river otters, birds, and even bats and butterflies that hung in shadow boxes on the walls. There was a wide variety of displays, from the terrifying to the ridiculous. A family of rats and several ducklings dressed like characters in a Beatrix Potter story were arranged on the window sill, as if looking out at the river that stretched in front of the house.

"Jessie loved the river view," Dad said. "That's part of her obsession with the animals. She collected all the animals you could see along the riverbank and in the yard. When she would tell stories about the White Lady of the River she would always say the animals could see and hear her anguished cries when no one else could."

Abby was familiar with the story, which had been told and retold at least twice a year since she could remember. Rowena, the beautiful raven-haired daughter of the mansion's original owner, apparently roamed the banks of the Holston, searching for her lost love, who had drowned in the river only hours before their wedding.

"Look at this one," her dad said, snapping Abby out

of her thoughts. "It was her favorite."

On the nightstand beside the ornate four-poster bed stood a grotesque hybrid creature. The body of a rabbit, right down to its cottony tail, had been paired with the head of a duck. Beside it stood an arrangement of mice, stuffed and dressed in Victorian mourning clothes.

Aunt Jessie had slept in here. Like, right beside them. *Who* would do that?

"Dad, why the hell would you want to stay in here?" Abby asked. Hysteria mounted in her voice, and she fought for control.

"*Language*, Abs. Language."

"I'm sorry, Dad, but this goes beyond the morbid fascination of an eccentric old lady. This is just creepy. Like, *unhealthy* creepy."

Her father laughed. "You have an overactive imagination, Abby. Plenty of people collect taxidermy. This house is filled with old relics of histories long dead and buried. And it's ours now. We can do what we want with it, and if the taxidermy freaks you out that much, we can redecorate."

Abby released a breath. Thank *God*. Living in a creepy old house was one thing. Sharing it with mounted animal corpses was another.

Happier than she had seen him in months, her dad yawned and stretched before pushing off the floor and flopping onto the bed like an excited kid. Abby laughed in spite of herself. She hadn't seen her dad like this in a long time. He was acting just shy of giddy.

"This room's mine," he said, "and it's late. We should probably get some sleep before the movers get here tomorrow. You're welcome to any of the rooms down the hall."

Abby nodded and turned toward the door.

"Hey, Abs, you know I love you, right?"

Her dad was looking at her with the strangest expression, like he was scared or suddenly filled with dread.

"Sure, Dad," she said. "Love you, too."

He smiled. "And don't go snooping around in the middle of the night. It's easy to get lost here in the dark."

"Okay," she said. "Night."

Abby wasn't sure why, but when she closed the door to the master bedroom, she felt more alone than she had ever felt in her life. More alone than the first time she'd found her mother...

Surrounded by unfamiliar pictures, strange drafts, and a feeling she couldn't shake, Abby wished for the small apartment she shared with Dad in Danville. But her life was here now. The sooner she accepted it, the sooner she could move on.

With a sigh and a final look around, she continued down the hall, poking her head inside each doorway until she found what she was looking for—another room with a view of the Holston River, which stretched out in front of the property like a tarry slough in the dark night.

Abby wondered if the lovelorn maiden from her father's stories had once stood in this very room in her youth, unaware that its view would be the source of so much pain.

Abby knew all about pain and loss. Maybe it's what drew her to the room.

Dock lights from nearby homes cast an eerie glow on the river's surface, the rapids foaming white as they crashed against rocks and branches. The view compelled Abby forward until she was standing in front of the window, staring out at the rushing current, made more tumultuous by the pounding rain. Abby was a strong swimmer. She had never feared the water before, but as it rushed down-stream, she couldn't help but shudder.

This is a river for drowning. A river for dying.

Shaking her head, Abby fought against the morbid thoughts. *Where had that even come from?* She repeated her father's promise aloud:

"Things will look brighter in the morning."

She took in the window seat that stretched the length of the wall and distracted herself by admiring the room. It was lined on either side with built-in bookshelves she would fill with all of her favorite novels once the moving truck arrived with the rest of their possessions in the morning.

This space was meant for her. She and her father would make this house their own, an oasis from everything they'd left behind in Kentucky.

For the first time, Abby was overcome by a sense of relief. New town. New house. New room. She could start over, be anyone she wanted to be. She wouldn't have to endure the whispers and the curious glances as she walked down the halls of a new school—at least, not for the same reasons as before. No one here had to know her mother had hated their lives in Danville so much she'd tried to end her own.

Somehow, amidst the gloom, excitement fought its way from her chest and bubbled up until Abby smiled. She dropped her bag on the trunk at the foot of the canopy bed and hopped up, falling back against the pillows. The mattress was soft at least. In the rain, though, the entire house smelled damp, the musty odor clinging to her skin and clothes like a lingering shadow.

You don't belong here.

Abby sat up, pushing back against the headboard. She looked around.

Had she said that out loud? Had it been her voice or someone else's echoing in her mind? She recalled the portrait of her dead aunt that loomed over the fireplace, those unforgiving eyes that could slice right through her. Maybe whatever trace of Aunt Jessie that remained was insulted Abby hadn't given the house the respect it deserved.

Laughing at the ridiculous thought, Abby hopped down and returned to the window seat, plopping down on the cushion to peer through the glass at the banks of the river.

Ever since the divorce, ever since her mother's hospitalization, Abby had felt like she herself was slowly losing her mind. She had hoped the new house would make things better. But now, she wasn't so sure it would.

Fog rose like a ghost from the murky water and hovered just over its surface for as far as she could see. Clouds covered the starless sky, which added to Abby's sudden sense of dread. Shaking it off, she started to turn away when a movement outside caught her eye.

A fluttering in the shadows.

Beside a lamp that illuminated a small section of the river, a figure walked slowly along the bank. A young woman with dark hair stared into the river as if searching for something lost. The dress she wore was timeless, with a corseted waist and a full taffeta skirt that swayed as she walked. A long gossamer veil whipped behind her in the wind as the woman wandered closer and closer to the edge of the river.

Abby pounded on the window to warn her away from the water, but the figure didn't hear against the pelting rain. She raised her fist to try again when a loud thud sent her whirling around, her heart pounding.

Her bag, weighted down by the few books she had forced inside with her clothes, had fallen to the floor behind her.

Releasing a breath and shaking her head, Abby turned back to the window. The woman was gone.

This is a river for drowning...

"You're totally losing it," Abby said to her reflection in the window pane.

A ghostly woman in a flowy white garment? Laughter burst from her lips at the absurdity of the cliché she had dreamed up.

Ghosts weren't real.

Houses weren't haunted.

Real horror was losing loved ones that couldn't be helped. It was in the maniacal wails of a mother who no longer knew her own daughter. Not in fictional stories created for the thrill of an adrenaline rush.

Abby was just tired. It had been a long drive through the rain and what felt like an even longer tour of the house. It was definitely time to clock out for the night. Grabbing her toothbrush from her overnight bag, Abby kicked off her shoes and wandered down the hall.

Two doors down, she found a large bathroom with a pedestal sink situated beneath an oval mirror. On the far wall, there was a toilet and a shower, across from a beautiful claw-foot tub that would be great for soaking.

But tonight, Abby was too tired to give it a try. She smeared the bright green paste onto her toothbrush and turned on the faucet. As she thoroughly brushed all the spots, she glanced in the mirror at her reflection.

Behind her, a twisted face snarled.

Empty eye sockets stared back at her, their bottomless depths anchoring Abby to the floor, holding her silent and still.

The toothbrush clipped Abby's gums and slipped through her hands. The creature behind her opened its mouth, brown, decayed teeth visible as it tried to speak. But suddenly, it choked. Water poured from its mouth and splashed to the floor.

Cursing, Abby jumped forward, nearly climbing onto the sink. Pain shot through her mouth. The toothbrush clattered to the floor. Shielding herself, she turned toward the figure she'd seen.

It was gone. Nothing but the empty space of the bathroom stared back at her.

Adrenaline surged through her veins, her pulse thumping in her ears. Abby tasted blood and toothpaste in her mouth, but she swallowed it back. On shaky knees, she knelt down and grabbed her fallen toothbrush with trembling hands. Her breath hitched in her throat as she tried to calm herself.

She was alone.

It was just her and Dad in the house.

No one else.

Nothing else.

But she couldn't shake what she had seen: black hair, thin and tangled, had streaked across a white face with skin that looked moldered against empty eye sockets. The lips had been as white as the face they adorned.

Abby closed her eyes against the image that would be branded into her memory forever. Tears pooled as the grotesque image morphed into the visage of her mother, lying still in a railed bed, her eyes vacantly staring ahead, seeing nothing and everything all at once.

Abby held her head in her hands, breathing in and out, in and out, fighting against her toxic fears. Shaking off the morbid thoughts, she sprinted down the hall and rounded the corner. But by the time she reached the master bedroom, she stopped.

This was all wrong.

She couldn't stay here.

They couldn't stay here.

She would wake Dad, and then they would leave, and that would be that.

But when she inched the door open, a slant of light from the hallway shone on the form of her sleeping father. Though stuffed pets and animals that had once roamed the grounds loomed over him like frozen specters, he slept soundly, his breaths coming out in even, restful puffs.

Her father who had barely slept since the divorce.

Her father who fought every day to keep it together for Abby's sake.

Even when her mother had cursed him, even when she had begged him to leave her, he still visited every single day without fail. Images of him sitting by her mother's bed and feeding her when she wouldn't lift an arm to feed herself swirled through Abby's memory. The smell of the fresh flowers he placed in colorful vases seemed to linger in the air even now, miles from the past. He had filled Mom's room with all of her favorites—yellow roses by her bed, white irises and snapdragons from her garden by the television, and African violets on the window sills.

Even when Abby had found him at their kitchen table halfway through a bottle of bourbon, his face still wet with tears as he held a pen over the documents with a shaky hand, he had still gotten up the next morning to cook Abby's breakfast. And though her stomach had been in knots, Abby had scraped her plate without tasting a single bite.

With a guilty breath, Abby turned from the room, dread rising in her throat. How could she tell him *she* was the one seeing things now? Things that couldn't be real.

Just like Mom.

She walked back down the hall and turned the corner toward her room. She would tell Dad everything tomorrow. And he'd know what to do.

She slipped beneath the cool blankets and pulled them up to her chin, recalling her last visit with her mother. It had been only a few days after her dad had met with the executor of Aunt Jessie's estate. Abby had been angry, had selfishly wanted to hurt Mom, despite her deteriorating mental state. She had waltzed into the room, turned off the TV her mother stared at all day, and announced that Aunt Jessie had died, that they were moving.

"Looks like you finally got your wish," Abby had said to her mother. "Dad and I are leaving, just like you wanted. We're moving to Aunt Jessie's mansion. You'll never have to see us again."

Abby would never forget the look in her mother's eyes— her mother, who had stared vacantly at the television or the ceiling and hadn't uttered a sound in weeks.

But now, her mother turned her head and looked at Abby, *really* looked at her. Her mother's expression was filled with terror, like a doe staring down the barrel of a hunting rifle. Tears had filled her eyes and spilled over.

Then, Mom had gripped her head and screamed.

Long, loud wails that echoed down the halls long after the nurses had pushed Abby away, and she had sprinted away from the room, from the building, and from her mother.

Abby choked back a sob. What if her mother's fate foreshadowed her own? What if she had inherited whatever tormented her mother?

"No," Abby said. "Everything will be okay tomorrow."

She repeated the words in her mind and listened to the steady pelting of rain against the window until she drifted away and thought no more.

• • •

*S*he stepped into the river, the icy water closing around her ankles like shackles. *What would it feel like? To take another step and then another and another? To allow the water to swallow knees, waist, shoulders? To fight the current and push toward the center of the water? Going deeper and deeper until the water numbed her skin and dulled her senses?*

Would she simply drift to sleep, the water cradling her like a mother?

Or would death sting like a blade? Perhaps it would linger like the never-ending sorrow of a solitary life...

The pain was too strong—too strong to bear.

The loss was too much.

She stepped over slick rocks, steadying herself against the current. Then, when the water reached her neck, she looked up at the sky, lifted her feet, and let it all go...

• • •

A bby lurched forward, gagging and coughing. She brought her hands to her throat as she gulped the air around her, swallowing it down like a starving animal until her lungs relaxed. The sound of her slowing breath resonated in her ears, her shoulders rising and falling violently until everything evened out. She placed her hands on either side of her hips, sinking into the soft mattress as she scooted back. It was just a dream.

Only it wasn't *just* anything.

It was the most vivid, terrifying nightmare she'd ever had. She could still smell the water, could still taste it in her mouth. She leaned back against the headboard, trying to calm down, when a cool breeze caressed her bare shoulders.

The window was wide open, the sheer curtains billowing toward her like waving arms.

Had she opened it?

No, she hadn't.

The rain had been rattling against the glass when Abby had climbed, terrified, into bed after her bathroom encounter.

The bedside lamp was off now, too. She had kept it on because she had been too afraid of the dark.

The wind lifted the curtains, causing their ends to snap together with a sound like a waving flag. She pulled the covers tightly against her chin and waited, never taking her eyes from the window as the dread threatened to close her throat.

Then, something wet splattered against her head and rolled down the back of her scalp. She reached up with a careful hand and touched the spot that had dampened her hair. When she examined her fingers, something dark and sticky clung to them. Her pulse thrumming in her ears, she looked up. A dark red stain had blossomed across the ceiling like a Rorschach and pooled in the center, falling in fat droplets—like steady tears.

Shaking, Abby threw the covers back and stumbled out of bed, trying to deny what was leaking down from the floor above. She stumbled toward the doorway, bracing herself on the frame, deciding which way to run.

Somewhere, in the distance, a pain-filled cry echoed through the empty hallway. Abby scampered back, pressing herself against the wall. She tried to slow her breathing, which was coming out in terrified gulps. She held herself up on wobbly knees and listened. The silence buzzed in her ears, and she could hear her heart knocking against her chest.

Whatever had made the sound was gone now. She released a controlled breath and pushed up from the wall. Gathering her wits, she peered into the dark hallway and crept along the floor runner, her legs still shaky. Fighting against a fear that left her trembling, she climbed the stairs.

She took one step, and then another and another, climbing higher and higher until she reached the third floor. Gripping the bannister, she tried to remember the location of her room on the floor below as she studied the hallway that stretched endlessly before her.

She had just taken a step forward when the squeak of a door hinge held her in place—suspended like one of the animals in her dad's room.

The third door on the left inched open, casting a sliver of light into the dark hall. Whispering voices echoed in the space around her. Then, she heard a distinct cry, loud and haunting. Someone wailing, as if in pain. Frozen in place, she took a deep breath, closing her eyes to gather her courage. She forced herself toward the room and slowly pushed wide the door.

Abby didn't know what she had expected to see, but she could never have prepared herself for the reality.

In the center of the room, a platform held a thick wooden post. Iron shackles hung down from the top, sending years of history lessons screaming through Abby's memory.

A whipping post.

Three ornate chairs formed a semi-circle around the platform, as if intended for an audience, which sent chills skittering up Abby's spine. She doubled over, gagging, as a sudden wave of nausea sent her stumbling forward.

She landed hard on the wooden floor, pushing up on all fours. Fighting against the dizziness, she looked up, her eyes locking onto a table in the back of the room.

Thunder rumbled outside, lightning from the storm illuminating some kind of altar. Thick pillar candles lined the table, along with heavy old books covered in dust. Abby forced herself to stand and crept closer, her footsteps creaking across the floor boards.

What the hell had happened in this house? What had Aunt Jessie been involved with?

Flashes of lightning revealed wall hangings and old drawings full of symbols Abby had never seen, along with familiar pentagrams and pentacles. Beside some kind of chalice or goblet were tiles labeled with ancient runes. A deck of tarot cards was stacked next to a pestle and mortar. Bundles of herbs were strewn about the table, their ends burned as if they'd been set on fire.

She'd seen enough movies to know this stuff was either used to summon evil or keep it at bay.

Too afraid to touch anything on the table, Abby hurried toward the door. She had to get to her father. They had to get out of this house *now*. Just as she passed the platform, a sickly odor rose up all around her. It smelled salty and metallic.

Like blood.

She stopped beside the whipping post and clenched her fists. Gathering every ounce of courage, she looked down at her bare feet. A dark stain was visible against the hardwood. Abby dropped to her knees, wiping her hand across the spot. It was totally dry.

But the smell was still there, pungent in her nostrils. The scent of fresh blood.

Everything connected.

The whipping post, the altar, the dried bloodstain on the floor, the agonized wailing that had echoed through the halls. Her father had told her stories of the sadistic overseer who had bought the plantation from the original owner. According to the legends, he had punished his slaves with a heavy hand until his own untimely death some years later.

Abby laughed as she rose to her feet, the sound echoing in the empty room. This was all in her mind. Childhood stories had risen to the surface of her subconscious to cause vivid delusions on her first night in this godforsaken mansion.

That was it. Nothing more.

And all the other weird items—the pentagrams and candles and freaky stuffed animals—were the remnants of an eccentric old lady who was clearly fascinated with the occult.

"You, girlfriend, are freaking losing it," Abby said to herself.

After chasing nonexistent horrors in the middle of the night, she needed to go tell Dad what was happening so they could take care of the problem. Abby just needed rest—and probably some mind-altering medication. Which was going to have to be strong if Dad expected her to live here.

No way was she going to end up like her mother.

She hadn't even made it to the door, though, when she heard someone singing:

I'm going down to the river of Jordan
Oh, yes,
I'm going down to the river of Jordan
Some of these days, Hallelujah...

Abby scrambled from the room, straining to hear the song.

Roll, Jordan, roll
I want to go to heaven when I die
To hear Jordan roll...

The voice was behind her, yet all around her, it seemed. Small and childlike.

She turned, moving swiftly toward the door, and peeked around the frame into the dark hall. A small figure, its edges blurred and obscured in a haze, disappeared as it neared the main stairs.

Confused, Abby followed it, the tune of the haunting song echoing in her mind. When she rounded the corner, though, the hall was empty.

She ventured further, pulsing adrenaline driving her to madness. She should turn around, she should wake Dad, but something, some unseen force, urged her forward.

She saw movement in the shadows ahead and followed the movement until she reached the edge of the main stairs. In the foyer, a woman moved across the marbled floors, her white taffeta dress crinkling as she glided forward, holding a candle. The lacy edge of her gossamer veil trailed behind her like webbing against the floor.

The woman Abby had seen walking along the river.

Abby shook her head. None of this was real. She was imagining it all.

Her breathing accelerated, increasing her heart rate. For a minute, Abby thought she might hyperventilate. She blinked again and again, but the woman was still there each time she opened her eyes again.

The mansion's front door opened with a creak. The woman stared straight ahead—straight toward the river, as though hypnotized, her raven-black hair blowing away from her pale face as the wind rushed through the door.

She moved forward, never turning from the river. A voice cried out in the distance before the sound of running water muffled it.

Rowena.

Had Abby heard that right? Rowena?

Abby thought back—was this the woman from the stories her father told? The woman whose restless spirit roamed the banks of the Holston, trying to reunite with her lost love?

Rowena. Yes, her name had been Rowena. She had lost her true love on the day of her wedding, and then, after years of unhappiness, she had walked into the icy waters never to be seen again.

"Rowena?" Abby whispered before she could bite back the words.

The woman suddenly stopped, straightening her spine.

Abby's head pounded along with her heart.

Slowly, the figure turned around. She regarded Abby with eyeless sockets, the black depths of them penetrating her soul like guilt. She had seen those same eyes only hours ago in the bathroom mirror.

She was sure of it.

"Rowena?" Abby whispered again.

When the woman opened her mouth to speak, water poured out instead of words. The putrid liquid rolled down her body, saturating her dress, and splattered against the marble of the floor as the woman stepped forward.

Then, there was water everywhere.

It rushed from her eye sockets, her ears and nose and mouth, as she tried to speak. She choked and gurgled against the words as she tried to form them.

Slowly, the her figure moved toward the stairs and began to climb, though she appeared to be drowning right in front of Abby.

Abby opened her mouth to scream, but her voice lodged in her throat.

She told her head to turn, her legs to move; she knew she needed to run away, but she was paralyzed, unable to look away from the watery, soulless depths of her empty eye sockets.

Then, the singing started again, echoing through Abby's mind like a terrible dream.

Jordan river's rolling
Cross it, I tell you, cross it
Cross Jordan's dangerous river...

Beside the woman, a child appeared. Shirtless and dressed in ragged brown pants, his dark skin marred by bloody slashes. He stared up at Abby with one eye. The other looked melted closed, as if he'd been blinded by something.

As if he'd been *branded*.

He opened his mouth and continued his song. Neither of the ghostly figures looking away from Abby, they slowly climbed the stairs.

Abby backed away, her entire body trembling.

"Dad!" Her voice rose barely over a whisper.

"Dad!" She was louder this time, but not loud enough.

Her heart—and the boy's song—blurred together in her ears. Along with a loud buzzing sound that sprang up somewhere behind her.

Afraid to turn from the two images in front of her—but more afraid of not knowing what was behind her—Abby whirled around. A tall, terrifying man holding a whip glared at her from the end of the hall. He held an old lamp and raised it until he was illuminated. His face was twisted, his eyes settled on the boy behind her, as if he were going to enjoy causing him pain.

The man opened his mouth as if to speak, but—as had been the case with the ghostly lady and the bloodied child—nothing came out.

Abby backed away as a single black fly crawled out of

his mouth. The buzzing grew louder.

The boy behind her raised his voice, singing louder. *Roll, Jordan, roll...*

As if provoked by the song, the man rushed forward, the toes of his boots dragging across the floor. He was so fast, Abby stumbled as he darted forth. A swarm of black flies burst from his mouth and surrounded her.

Then, she was falling, propelled backward by a rush of cold as the man collided with her...or *through* her, rather. The flies buzzed like static in her ears.

She never felt the impact of the fall.

When she opened her eyes, she was in the foyer, staring up at the three lost souls that loomed over her. Water from the drowning woman splashed over her with a putrid odor that forced a gag from Abby's throat.

The boy's wounds bled as if freshly opened, and a fat grub worm inched out of his ear and slithered around his head.

Then, the man with the whip was dragging Abby unrepentant, flies crawling out his eyes ears, nose, and mouth.

No! No! No!

Abby fought against him, but couldn't break free. All three figures were now restraining her. A moment later, she was being lifted.

As she struggled against their icy hands, the portrait in the adjacent room caught her eye. Aunt Jessie watched with piercing eyes.

Just like your mother. You don't belong here.

As the hands dragged Abby from the entryway, she cast a final glance at Aunt Jessie, the woman's cruel gaze showing no mercy, her thin lips slightly upturned in a cold smirk.

Cold rain pelted against Abby's bare skin as she was dragged out into the night, into the raging storm. Her tormentors jostled her past the towering shrubs and down the grand stone stairs. She screamed, cried out for her father, but the sound was drowned out by the deep rumble of thunder and the rushing of the river.

When her captors reached the grass, they dropped her on the ground, dragging her by her ankles. She rolled on her belly, digging her nails into the soft, wet earth. She clawed at the mud, trying to hold on, but they were too strong. Flies drifted from the buzzing man and landed on her arms.

The boy continued his song:

Roll, Jordan, roll
I want to go to heaven when I die
To hear Jordan roll...

Abby screamed, catching glimpses of the living dead as she thrashed about. They were waist deep in the rushing waters of the Holston. She cried out again, looking up at the house. A movement in the windows caught her eye. She blinked it into focus. Her father stood in one of the rooms, illuminated by soft light coming from behind.

He looked out at her from the open window, staring trance-like at Abby's struggle, touching the glass as if to say goodbye. Behind him, another figure appeared—tall and lean, standing straight as an iron post.

"Daddy!" Abby was screaming now, desperate. The river's icy water soaked through her clothes and clung to her skin.

Her fingers clenched fistfuls of mud. She dug her fingers into the soft earth. A fingernail snapped against a rock, though she didn't feel the pain. Flies buzzed in her ears as they leapt from her damp skin.

"Daddy, no!"

The figure behind her father drifted closer, her white hair swept up in a high bun. The gleam of a wooden cane caught the light. The long bony fingers of her hand came to rest on Dad's shoulder.

Never taking his eyes from Abby, her father drew back from the glass and placed his hand over Aunt Jessie's.

Then he smiled.

I was always her favorite.

With a sob, Abby turned away, images of her mother speeding through her memory.

Her mother had been here before she got sick.

She slid down the banister like a little girl…I don't think Aunt Jessie thought it was too funny…

The voice came back to Abby again—the one she'd heard moments ago, before being dragged outside.

Just like your mother. You don't belong here.

No! She wouldn't go out this way. She wouldn't end up like her mother.

Abby flipped over on her back, kicking and flailing against the dead hands that held her. She twisted and screamed, flies swarming her damp skin and buzzing low in her ears. She fought until she was breathless, until she was exhausted.

Until the boy's song gurgled and fell silent.

Roll...Jordan...

Water soaked her skin and clothes, the back of her head. Abby looked up into the night sky, squinting against the rain, and wondered what her mother had been trying to say through her hysterical screams that last day. Abby sobbed, crying out in desperate wails of anguish.

The ghostly woman in white loomed over her, water still gushing from the sockets of her eyes. She brought her index finger to her gray lips, as if to quiet Abby's struggling against the frigid current.

This is a river for dying.

A river for drowning.

As the current swallowed her, the water cradling her like a mother, Abby stopped crying.

She stared into the woman's eyes—into the black depths—lifted her feet, and let it all go.

BEKAH HARRIS was born and raised in the mountains of East Tennessee, where she has been writing since she could hold a pencil. The beauty of her home in the Appalachian Mountains, along with the legends, myths, and folklore of that area, is what inspires the unique plots and settings captured in her young adult fiction. In addition to her love of all things fictional, Bekah is also a high school English teacher and freelance editor. When not working, Bekah can be found at home building block towers for her son to knock down, as well as drinking coffee and watching Netflix with her husband.

WAMPUS

TRACY SUE NEEDHAM

Granny used to tell me the story of the night I was born. She said, "It come on quick-like, and there was no stopping it," even though she tried hard because I was a bit too early and "should have baked longer."

Epsom salts, wild yam root, black haw, she tried them all, but apparently I was stubborn and determined.

Some things never change.

Granny sent Daddy out to the wood pile to bring the axe, hoping to slide it under the bed to cut the pain, but in the blizzard, it couldn't be found. There wasn't time to look for it or anything else. It was at the stroke of midnight that I arrived. She pulled me from the caul with a gush of red waters and into the world I came, feet first.

My Momma, Sadie Rose, was always a delicate flower of a woman, I'm told, and the strain proved too much for her. Granny spit on my head and rubbed it with a coin from Daddy's pocket before placing a kiss on my forehead and wrapping me tightly in one of the little blankets that she and Momma had made.

As she laid me in the drawer for safe keeping, Momma slipped from this world.

Now, I don't know how much you know about superstitions and babies, but there were many things about my birth that raised warning flags for Granny. A baby born at midnight can see and hear spirits. A firstborn child is protected from witchcraft. A baby born with a caul is good luck, and if the waters are red, the child will have great powers and double sight. A baby born feet first will have healing abilities. So, she knew from the start she would have to keep her eyes on me. She swore I was meant to be the next healer.

My name is Oakley Apple Jackson—yes, really— but they used to call me Apple Jacks for short. I know, it sounds like an unusual name for a girl, but I always kind of liked it. Oakley was my momma's maiden name, Apple was Granny's Christian name, and of course Jackson was our family name.

That's what is most important around here: family.

As I drove back to the old mining town that was my

ancestral home, my mind was on my grandmother. Her name was Apple Sadie Oakley, but it had been years since she had been called anything but Granny Apple. She was the town's midwife, so half of those living there now had made their way into the world through her hands, and I was no exception.

Most of the Granny Women were gone now. Laws had prohibited their practices some years ago, though many would still swear by them.

The Granny Women were healers—a combination of herbalism, superstition, common sense, and witchcraft. It was an ancient heritage, passed from mother to daughter, from a blend of Old World, Native American, and all that made up the proud people of the Hills.

Granny had passed that knowledge down to me, and it would not be lost. Even with that doctorate that was about to hang on my wall, I could still see the value of Granny's ways. As Granny used to say, "All that book learnin' don't mean nothing without some good ole horse sense to go with it."

It had been Granny that raised me. Well, Granny and Momma's ghost.

My Daddy, he put in long hours at the mine and wasn't around all that much, since he was too busy trying to make a living for us. Life in the mines was back-breaking, tiring work.

When I wasn't at school, in the one-room class that was held in the church building in town, I would spend my days helping Granny with the housework or her patients. The nearest doctor was three towns over and a good two hours away, so Granny was the closest thing we had to medical care most days.

That was how I grew up, taking care of people. Granny taught me to grow simples—those are herbs used for medicines and to make home remedies. I learned everything from removing warts with Mayapple, to treating heart trouble with Foxglove, and about a hundred things in between. It's useful stuff to know, but Granny said not everybody had a knack for it. She always said that I come by it honestly, having both blood and magic on my side.

"You were born to it," she said.

Sometimes Momma's ghost would help me with learning the chores and such if Granny was busy. Mostly she taught me things like sewing and quilting; those were her favorite things to do when she was living.

Anywhere else, people might have looked at you funny if you were walking along, talking to a ghost, but here, most people understood that sort of thing—at least the older ones did.

For me, Momma was a lot like anyone else, except for not needing to eat or sleep and never getting any older.

When I was younger, I thought everybody could see Momma. I learned different once I went to school, though. The kids would laugh and tease me for talking to myself so much. I didn't understand why they couldn't see her. She was right there!

Vernard Martin would tease me 'til I couldn't stand it.

I remember the day it went too far, and I had enough of it. I hit him and took off, running all the way home. I was crying so hard as I ran that by the time I reached the house, I was nearly choking on my tears as I tried to catch my breath. Granny took me into the house, sat me down, and wiped my face with a cold cloth.

"I ain't never seen a'body so worked up, child. What be the meanin' of this here clatterment?" Granny asked.

It took me a few minutes of trying before I could choke out an answer. "That ignorant Vernard Martin was eavesdroppin' on my talkin' to Momma. Then he said I was queer and called me dumber than a coal bucket for believin' in haints, so I slugged him one and then skedaddled back here before I got into trouble."

Granny laughed.

That just made me madder and I stomped my foot, crossing my arms over my chest while screaming at her, "It's not funny!"

Granny knew it was serious to me, so she tried to contain her amusement. "That boy just be sparkin' on you is all, girl. He picks at you 'cause he likes you."

I looked at her like she'd grown an extra head. "He does not, Granny!" I protested, completely mortified at the idea. "He's a plumb fool!"

"It ain't his fault, child. Not every person can see a haint, let alone have a talkin' with one. You're different. Special. Not everybody can do what you can."

"Well, I think that mean old Vernard is a piece of

work, and if he devils me again, I'll snatch him bald!"

Granny just laughed as she gave me that look that suggested she knew something that I didn't.

The mountains where I grew up were full of stories of creatures, ghosts, and all kinds of things that go bump in the night—or in some cases, even in the day—and Granny loved to tell stories. You know the kind: those far-fetched wives' tales that only grow more and more unbelievably outlandish as they're passed from person to person, like a game of intergenerational Chinese telephone.

She had several of those.

When I was younger I would sit at her feet for hours, snapping beans or holding her ball of yarn as she knitted and told me the old legends. Back then, it never occurred to me to question if they were real. After all, Grandma said so, so it must be true. Right?

It was better than TV; but then again, we didn't have TV, so we wouldn't have known what we were missing if it wasn't.

I remember her favorite tale in particular; it was this story that she called "The Wampus Cat."

Most often she would tell it when I had done something that got me into some trouble, one way or another, like the day that I had tried to follow Daddy to the mines to see what they did there.

Daddy drug me back home and left me with Granny, who sat me down on the front porch and took a seat in her rocking chair. She picked up her knitting, and for a while we had sat there without her saying a word. I was waiting for a scolding, but one never came. Instead, she told me the Wampus Cat story.

• •

Way back a long time ago when the Cherokee lived in these mountains, there was a beautiful young Indian maiden. She had long, flowing black hair and big brown eyes full of curiosity.

Every morning she would make breakfast for her husband and ask him about his plans for the day, but he would never tell her anything. It was forbidden for women to know the secret rituals and magics of the tribe.

He would leave her to do the gardening and tend the house while he went off with the men. And when he came home, she would ask him how his day was.

Again, he would tell her nothing.

So, one day, when the woman couldn't stand wondering anymore, she decided that she would find out for herself what the men did every day. She took the hide of a cougar that had been skinned and wrapped herself in it as a disguise. Like a cat, she stalked them, following behind and hiding in the shadows 'til they stopped at the ritual grounds.

Crouching in the bushes, she lay low against the ground, her body hidden beneath the cat's skin as she stared out through the holes where it's eyes had once been, trying to see what was *happening in the clearing.*

As she watched, the men donned their ceremonial headdresses and began to chant while they danced around the fire the younger men had built.

Too far away to hear them clearly, she tried hard to listen, but no matter how she strained to hear, she could not make out the words of their chants, and so she crept forward, moving even closer to where she was not allowed to be.

Paying more attention to the men than to her own steps, a branch snapped under her as she crawled. The maiden pressed herself to the ground, willing herself to disappear so that she would not be noticed.

But it was too late.

The Shaman raised his hands and the group stopped, falling silent. The maiden held her breath as he extended his arm, his finger pointing to the spot where she lay.

She tried to run, but the men were quicker and she was easily caught. They drug her into the center of the circle, tearing the cougar skin from her and throwing her onto her knees before the waiting Shaman.

Her husband turned his back on her, refusing to acknowledge her or witness her fate.

The Shaman raised his staff and began to chant as the maiden cried and begged. As the men watched, the skin she had used to disguise herself rose up over her body and loomed above her. The maiden fell forward onto her hands and knees as she pleaded for mercy while the skin lowered slowly and settled onto her flesh, binding itself to her, transforming her into a beast.

..

Do you keen my meaning, child?" Granny had asked me once her tale was finished.

"Don't be so nosy?" I had said. Granny smiled and nodded, then handed me her yarn to hold as we again sat in silence, the only sound the clacking of her knitting needles.

I think I was about thirteen when the dreams and visions first started. Granny called it "the sight" and said that she'd been waiting for it to announce itself. She said that it often makes its presence known when a girl becomes a woman, and it came in screaming.

I woke up just as the sun rose one morning, drenched in sweat and shaking. I screamed for Daddy, but it was Granny that came. She told me that Daddy had already left for the mines.

I sprang out of bed and nearly fell down the ladder from the loft as I hurried after him. Running outside in my nightgown and bare feet, I tripped and fell. Granny reached me and helped me to my feet, taking me inside and cleaning me off. I begged her to let me go tell Daddy the horrible things I had dreamt. Before I could tell her about the nightmare, the church bells began to ring.

With so much distance between houses, the church bells were used to communicate things to the entire area. Short or long rings, various combinations—they all meant different things.

Listening closely, we could tell that these bells meant something was very wrong down at the mines.

Granny grabbed her bag, and I tugged on my dress. We headed to the mine as fast as we could, but it was too late. There were flames coming from the entrance, just like I had seen in my sleep.

Daddy didn't come out.

The others said he was a hero and helped them to escape. They looked for him, but I could already see him standing beside Momma.

• • •

The years after that were pretty quiet. I studied hard, and the teacher helped me get a grant to go away to college. The whole town pitched in what money they could to buy my train ticket, and they all gathered to see me off. I promised to come home soon as I headed off to the big city to become a doctor.

But I grew up and lost that sense of mysticism and wonder. I left the mountains and their ways behind me. The dreams and visions seemed to have been lost and the ghosts had forgotten me.

For years I planned on visiting, coming home, but life has a habit of getting in the way. Working as a waitress took time away from my studies, plus I was saving up to buy a car.

I put off visiting for too long.

Last night, I had been in my room at college and had dozed off while studying. The dream came to me then. Granny, her eyes wide in fear, clutched at her chest as she dropped to the floor and lay there, slumped over, lifeless. I immediately headed out, but I knew I would be too late. I could feel it as the car neared the familiar edges of town. Her spirit had left her body.

I turned the car off of the main road and started the long drive to the cabin. Gifts were stronger here in the mountains. There was something in the earth there—a deep connection to the land and the people who live on it. I could feel it inside me. It had called me home.

The town was set down in the holler. Everything looked the same as it had five years ago. Nothing really changed much here anymore. Most people had moved out once the mines closed, going wherever they could find work. A few remained, like Granny, either retired or living off the land.

It was still home.

Some familiar faces spoke with me as I drove slowly down Main Street. Rose Johnson waved from the stoop of the general store; I knew from Granny's letters that she owned it now.

Miss Jackson, an old spinster cousin, was sweeping the steps of the schoolhouse where she was still teaching. Little Opal's ghost skipped along beside my window, chattering about how much she missed me as

I headed towards the nighway to Granny's house.

It was a well-worn path, as many still sought her for herbs and teas and such. No one mentioned her being gone. Maybe I was wrong, or maybe nobody knew it yet. I was hoping for the first one.

I parked the car at the end of the path and started on foot towards the old house. Granny lived so far back in the woods that—as they say—you had to pipe sunshine in.

Things seemed wrong. It was just too quiet. During the day, the path was normally a beautiful walk, though at night it could get hainty. I wondered where the birds were.

I felt like something was watching me as I neared the house and passed it off as maybe a ghost knew I was here. Over the years, I'd come to learn that ghosts were mostly just lonely, and if you could see them, they were more than happy to talk to you.

I jumped a bit. It was just the breeze in the trees. I was probably making a mountain out of a molehill, as Granny would say.

At the front porch, I hesitated. The leather britches hanging from the roof were still, so no breeze was blowing. But the empty rocking chair rocked regardless. I knew I wasn't wrong. I could feel the eyes on me, watching. Granny's and something else's.

I stepped onto the porch. Her knitting needles lay in a partially-made blanket atop the basket holding her yarn. She wasn't in the chair. I pushed open the door and hollered, "Granny?"

No answer. My heart rose up into my throat as I stepped inside. It was dark and still. The death watch beetle was silent. A cold chill swept over me, and I shivered.

In the front room, the fire had died out in the fireplace and a quilt was stretched across the frame. Looking closer, I recognized the pattern—a double wedding ring—and wondered who was getting married.

In the kitchen, a pot of beans was set to soak, all the water drawn up.

In the bedroom, the bed was made. My room looked just like I had left it all those years ago.

Granny was nowhere to be seen.

"Sadie!" I called, hoping to scare up Momma's ghost.

No answer. I tried calling her from my room.

"Momma?"

Still nothing.

Tossing my backpack onto the bed, I checked the bathroom just in case, before heading out to the back-yard, where there was an old root cellar that Granny still used to store canned goods, vegetables, and smoked meats. The door was unbolted. I felt my heart clutch and I ran, oblivious to being watched or the tracks outside, leading beneath the door. I ripped it open and screamed.

Granny laid there on the dirt floor surrounded by glass and bread n' butter pickles. I let out a wail as I ran to her, the doctor in me taking over as I reached to feel for a pulse in her neck, but the witch in me knew it was too late.

Letting out a keen, I sat in the mess on the floor and pulled her body into my arms, rocking as I sobbed. I saw her spirit as she stepped from the shadows, watching me cradle her corpse. She looked terrified. Her finger pressed against her lips, shushing me, as I started to speak, and my eyes followed her as she moved towards the corner where she kept the meats after they had been smoked.

Eyes glowed back at me from the darkness, and I froze.

Round eyes, a deep brown—familiar, but wild and feral.

I could hear whatever it was panting as it watched me. Through my own terror, I could still feel what it felt— frightened, cornered, lonely...

As my eyes focused, I was more confused. It had cat-like ears and whiskers, tawny fur. The teeth looked razor sharp and blood-stained. Pieces of raw meat still clung to them. It moved towards me, and I held my breath.

The creature stood up on two legs and walked outward form the dark corner toward us.

I clutched Granny's lifeless body closer, protecting her what little I could, as the creature moved between us and the door. As it stood in the light, I could see it clearly.

It looked more like a cougar, but the eyes were wrong. It looked at me with what I can only describe as human curiosity. Granny's stories flooded back to me as I watched it coming closer, and fear coursed through my whole body.

I felt like I was being studied as it looked me over and made a cat-like hissing sound. I swallowed hard, my head trying to override my fear.

"Shoo!" I yelled at the thing. "Go!"

It looked like I had wounded it, and just then it let out a howl that sent a shudder through me, chilling me to the bone. I grabbed a jar from the shelf and threw it. Hitting the cellar wall beside the creature's head, it shattered, pieces of glass and pickled beets flying everywhere. The cat creature made a wounded sound and dashed for the open door, fleeing. I tried to take a deep breath, fighting to let my rational mind take over as I knelt there, trembling with grief and fear.

Gently, I laid her body back down as Granny's ghost soothed me.

"It's okay child. Get yerself together now. I be fine. She just skeer the livin' daylights clean out of me was all. I done lived a long one; 'twas nigh on time. Who'd a thunk it's be the ole Wampus Cat!

"Now git yerself up out of that mess, and I'd be much obliged if'n you'd be gettin' me out of them pickles, too."

Despite myself, I laughed and, shaking my head, made my way back out of the cellar, already going over a list of things to do in my mind before I started into town again.

Granny never had put in a phone and my cell phone

didn't get reception out here, so I had to start back on foot. The sheriff's office was back in town, just about a fifteen-minute walk or so. I hurried, though there wasn't much point in it.

I stepped in the door, out of breath, and looked up to see Vernard Martin seated behind the desk, reading a book. He jumped, startled as the door slammed behind me, and I stood there panting.

"Hey, Jacks, didn't know you were home. What's got you riled?" I had gone to school with Vernard—Bear, we always called him—most my life.

"Granny's dead, Bear. I need you to come up to the house."

He took off, like he'd been shot, out of the chair. Granny was special to a lot of folks, him included. She'd delivered him when he was born and nursed him through a bad fever spell that nearly took him when we were young—not to mention countless bouts of the molly-grubs. He grabbed his bag and a set of keys from the hook beside me. "Let's go."

We took the four-wheeler back, me riding behind him and hanging on tight as he flew through the woods. It might have been fun if it hadn't been for Granny being dead. I took him to see where she was; he made notes and took some pictures for the report.

After he finished, Vernard came to stand beside me, awkwardly looking at the ground, his toe digging into the dirt.

"Uh, Jacks, how do you want to do this? Are you

thinkin' local, or do you want me to call the folks at the city funeral home?"

For a moment, I couldn't believe that he would even ask such a thing. "No, Bear, there is no way that Granny would want that. You know she would want the old ways near as we can."

"You're right, of course. Tell me how I can help."

I thought about it for a moment, mentally working on the list of what needed to be done.

"We will lay her out in the front parlor. I can tend her from there. We will need to get ahold of the coffin maker and let people know."

"I'll help you get her inside and then start notifying people for you. The rest of the statement can wait till later; Granny's more important right now. Let's get her tended first."

"Thanks, Bear. I'm glad you're here."

"Anything for you, Jacks."

I sent him to get the laying-out board from the old shed, and he put it in the parlor between two chairs. Then, he picked Granny up and carried her like a baby in his arms, bringing her in to lay her down on it. I didn't tell him her ghost was behind him, scolding the whole way. Granny did tend to be a little bossy when it came to the rituals.

"Hey now, careful, I ain't no sack o' potatoes! Girl, tell that lad to watch my head!"

I followed behind them, trying to ignore her as she kept talking.

"So's you be knowin' to the circumstance, Vernard-boy ain't sparkin' anyone."

I rolled my eyes at her as she gave it out and mumbled out of his earshot, hoping he wouldn't hear, "I'm no play-perty out spreein'. Really now! Sheesh.'"

This time it was Granny's turn to roll her eyes at me. "Get on it then, girl."

"I can handle my own love life, thank you very much. And I would really rather not be arguing this with you right now. You know how Vernard is about me talking to haints!'"

It was really quite out of whack to be arguing with a ghost while you laid her body out.

I stepped ahead of Vernard and held the door open for him as he carried Granny's body through it and into the parlor. Following behind him again, I made a shushing gesture back to Granny, putting my finger to my lips where he couldn't see.

Once Vernard had laid her corpse onto the board for me, helped me to tie her down with sheets to keep it straight, and made sure I was okay, he headed back into town. Just because I was capable of handling things alone didn't mean that I would have to. You see, around here death brings folks together, and no one has to go through grieving alone. That just isn't our way.

As soon as he left, I started drawing the curtains and covering the mirrors. Not that it would work, you see; the purpose was to close off the glass so that it couldn't be used as a portal for the dead person's ghost, and they could cross over to their new life without looking back. I turned all the clocks back to the time I had felt her die and stopped them there. Time stood still for her now, but in my heart I knew she had no intention of leaving anytime soon anyway.

Still, tradition was tradition.

I lit the fire and the candles. It was getting late, and with everything closed, the house grew dark fast.

I chose her Sunday best from her closet and set it in the parlor before taking stock of what I required. The herbs cabinet was in the kitchen, so I looked through, gathering the ones I needed.

Opening the shed to gather more things, I heard the church bell ring.

I wondered who was in charge of that. Whoever they were, they would be ringing for a long time. The bell would peel once for every year of Granny's life. People would be counting the rings so they knew who it might be, though some would start coming by the church to hear the news. The women would begin arriving here soon. Briefly, I wondered how many remembered the old ways as I carried my things inside, leaving the door unbarred.

Lovingly, I washed the body, coating it with a balm before perfuming it and dressing it in a traditional black. Carefully, I crossed her arms on her chest and tied her stockinged feet together at the ankles. Tears filled my eyes as I wrapped the scarf about her face, to keep her mouth closed, and pulling two quarters from my pocket, I closed her eyes, weighting the lids.

The first of the visitors began to arrive. I greeted them, thanking them for coming, and one by one they pitched in. Things would move quickly. Without arterial embalming, the body doesn't keep; the topical would only hold so long.

The first ones to arrive were the Archers. They lived the closest. Henry Archer was my age and had married my high school best friend, Becky Rae Martin. She was Vernard's sister. Becky tried to set me down with a cup of tea, but I wouldn't have it. Henry's parents, Jesse and Sally Anne, were with them, as well as his grandma, who they called Lala. I didn't know her given name.

Lala had been Granny's best friend since they were little. She wasn't walking so well these days, but she took pride in handing me the pot of stew they'd brought along and insisted on helping me finish dressing the body. I let her do up Granny's hair and finally agreed to Becky's cup of tea, watching as Granny's ghost stood over Lala.

She was stubbornly supervising her own laying out—not that Lala could hear her. I just shook my head and walked away, trying not to giggle.

Later, some men came with a wagon carrying the coffin. Apparently Granny had already had it made for when the time came. Somehow I wasn't surprised. It was a simple pine box covered in black linen with a soft lining of lavender cotton. Granny loved lavender.

They lifted her from the board and settled her gently inside. It was very reverent and somber work. Then, the coffin was placed back up onto the chairs.

On an impulse, I brought in dried lavender from the porch and handed it to Lala, who smiled as she wove it into the braids of Granny's hair before fastening a posy. As she looked around for something to bind it with, I pulled the ribbon from my own hair and handed it over for her to use, a small but symbolic gesture. Lala slid the little bouquet beneath the hands as they rested against Granny's chest.

Suddenly I realized that the saining was up to me, since I was the oldest woman of the family now.

Everything was quiet as I gathered the things that I would need for the ritual. I joined Lala at the side of the coffin and lit the candle before passing it over Granny's body three times as I said the blessings.

Handing the candle to Lala, I then measured three handfuls of salt into a little wooden bowl before placing it on the corpse's chest. This would protect her body from harm and keep it from rising unexpectedly.

Granny was ready now.

Leaving her friends with her, I slipped out to the porch to drink my tea in Granny's rocking chair. Becky had obviously taken a sachet from Granny's herb box, because the chamomile mint was her own favorite homemade blend.

Vernard came back just as I sat down and closed my eyes a moment. I sipped the tea as we talked. He seemed a bit shy suddenly as he said, "I missed you, Jacks," and I suddenly felt flushed and warmer than the tea could have made me.

"It's been a long time, Bear," I stammered. There was a tense silence as our eyes met before we awkwardly looked away and his hand covered mine.

He sat quietly with me for a few moments, his hand still on mine before going over the report, telling me that the tracks were strange and asked me what I had seen. I gazed at him a moment as I considered how to answer, not sure he would believe me if I told him the truth.

Looking him in the eye, I started to speak as I set my cup into the saucer with a shaky hand. "It was the Wampus Cat. I saw her, Bear."

I no sooner said the name before we heard it, that ungodly screech of a wild cat, but eerier.

The teacup shattered at my feet as I shook, and Vernard's hand went to his gun.

Granny's ghost shot out into the woods so quick I almost didn't see it happen, and I screamed, my legs going weak as my body lowered to the ground, unable to support myself.

Henry and his daddy were on the porch quicker than a drunk man feathered into a free-for-all. Vernard pulled me to my feet and pushed me into the house, pulling the door closed behind him.

The cat screeched again, nearer this time, and the women huddled together, closer to the fire, as I banged at the door that Vernard had closed in my face. "You can't kill it!" I wailed as I pounded, sinking down to my knees and sobbing. I babbled like a crazy person, and I screamed through the door that they needed to come back. Becky wrapped her arms around me and half-drug me over to the fire with the rest of them.

I clung to her and pleaded, "Please Beck, they don't understand, they don't know, they can't kill it. It's not what they think!"

We could hear the creature outside the house, pacing, trying to get inside. Becky tried to tell me it was just a cougar, and I sobbed.

Then Lala, who'd been calm and quiet, spoke up. As the creature stalked us, Lala began to explain why I was so upset for those who hadn't heard or didn't remember.

"You saw her, didn't you chile?"

I nodded.

"And you know, don't you? You know what she is?"

I nodded again, drying my tears on the quilt stretched across its rack.

There came another screech as the door rattled, and I rushed to it, dragging Becky with me. Together we slid the bar into its cradle, securing the door.

On impulse, I ran for the herb cabinet; rummaging through it, I came up with basil and rosemary before pulling nine straws from the broom. I handed Becky the straws and rosemary.

"Into the fire, rosemary first, then the straws, slowly, one at a time!" I instructed.

As she started, I dashed about, tying the dried basil to the window sills and doors. I snatched the salt and carried it with me, nabbing the jar of moonshine from the counter along the way.

Settling in on the floor once more, I sprinkled salt around us before cracking open the shine and taking a deep swig. I coughed as I handed it to Becky, and she drank before passing it along.

Together we shared it, from person to person, as Lala began the story again and the beast paced about us, scratching at the doors and windows and making the meowls of an angry cat.

"That there is no cougar," Lala said. "It is a creature called the Wampus Cat. She is a Cherokee woman who done been cursed to walk the mountains in the *skin* of a cougar. The men captured her and drug her into the circle, still wrapped in the skin that she had tried to hide herself in. As punishment for breakin' the rules, the medicine man cast a spell that caused the skin to bind to her flesh, locking her into the cat's form for all time.

"She is forever denied the company of people and beast, being neither one or the other, and is doomed to wander up and down the Appalachians alone. She steals food and kills men, frightens the life out of women and children, stalking them.

You've heard that curiosity killed the cat—well now y'be knowin' why."

I spoke softly then.

"I saw her. She had these eyes that looked so sad and lonely. She was terrified. I don't think she meant to hurt anyone. She was trapped. I think Granny surprised her while she was stealing meat from the cellar, and they got stuck when the door blew shut. Granny's heart gave out from the scare.

"The Wampus Cat didn't kill Granny. But I don't know why she's still hanging around."

Then I realized.

"Oh no!" I jumped to my feet and ran, struggling to unbar the door. Before they could stop me, I rushed onto the porch and cried out into the night. "I'm sorry! I didn't mean to threaten you! I didn't know it would hurt you for me to talk the way I did to you. Please, no one here can hurt you."

Then, as hard as it was to say it, as much as I missed Granny, I said, "I know it was an accident."

I stood shivering in the cold mountain air as I looked out into the night. Everything went quiet and still as I trembled there on the porch, hoping she would understand.

From the dark, those eyes appeared. I saw them coming close to me. Determined to show her I was sincere, I stood my ground. She stalked closer, moving sleekly, catlike.

Then as she entered the light, she rose up onto her back legs, walking like a human, soundlessly closing the gap between us.

I reached my hand out before me, turning the palm up, like one would to a pet to show no harm. My eyes met hers, and I felt the emotion in them as I had earlier—so lonely, so hurt, so broken. She only wanted to understand.

The huge paw raised as she placed it on top of my palm, and we stood there without a word. I swear a tear rolled down her cheek as she gripped her toes gently around my fingers. For that brief moment, we understood each other.

Then a third hand settled atop hers as Granny's ghost appeared beside us. She leaned to press a kiss to the Wampus Cat's forehead and whispered in her ear, "It was my time; it's not your fault."

Slowly drawing back her paw, the cat turned and fled back into the woods as the men entered the clearing.

Granny's ghost settled into her rocker as Vernard took my hand. "We didn't find anything. The cougar must have cleared out with all the people. It should be safe again, at least for now—say, is that chair rocking by itself?"

I just shook my head and, still holding onto Vernard's hand, led them inside, promising to tell him about it later. Although she had gone, I could still feel those yellow eyes watching me from a distance.

But it was okay, I told myself.

She was just curious.

TRACY SUE NEEDHAM was born in Northwest Indiana and spent much of her adult life traveling the United States before settling in the Wyoming Valley of Pennsylvania, where she lives with her ginger tabby cat, Napoleon. She began writing poetry as a child and published her first piece in the fifth grade. Participation in the #ThingADay618 artist's project rekindled her love of writing and has encouraged her to embark on new projects. Tracy Sue is making her fiction debut in *Witches of the Wood*.

CAROLINE

J. WARREN WELCH

The campfire popped and crackled as Andrew sat on a log, sipping a lukewarm cup of coffee. The top of Unaka Mountain was all grays and greens as the day slowly disappeared between the tall spruce trees that stretched toward the steadily darkening sky.

Andrew knew he was somewhere near the Tennessee and North Carolina border, but he'd been out on the Appalachian Trail for so long at this point that things like borders and states just seemed silly to him. Superfluous. This was all God's country, and God felt a great deal closer out here in nature, far away from the business and *busy*ness of mankind.

The middle-aged man looked older than he really was. The years of living this secluded, nomadic lifestyle had not been kind to him, but he felt safer out here.

And he knew he could never go back.

His eyes were tired, and his unshaven face was covered in hair that made him appear more homeless than hipster.

Andrew pulled a small New Testament from the breast pocket of his worn OD green coat.

He had to travel light out here, so he didn't carry a full copy of the Good Book, but the New Testament was always the part that gave him the most comfort anyway.

There was a lot of love in that story. Forgiveness. Grace. Truly amazing grace.

He read a few of his favorite passages about the blood of Christ washing away his own wrongdoings so that he could stand before a perfect God one day and be judged—as if he had never done anything wrong.

Never.

Andrew smiled at that beautiful thought.

"That saved a wretch like me..." Andrew whispered to himself as he closed the small, worn book and put it back in his breast pocket.

All traces of daylight had finally been swallowed up by the thick, dark mountain night that Andrew's small fire struggled to cast some light into. He twisted to his left to grab another piece of firewood.

When he turned back, there was a young girl standing directly on the other side of the campfire.

She wore a blue dress with a white ribbon tied around her waist, and another white ribbon tied in a bow that held her dirty-blond hair back. Her eyes were sunken into her pale face and her lips were a dark blue. She looked to be nine or ten years old. The front of her dress was smeared with what appeared to be wet blood, which glistened in the light of the flames from the fire.

"Holy fuck!" Andrew shouted as he fell backwards off the log, and then struggled to get to his feet and face the child. "Where did you come from?"

"You pray to your God with that mouth?" a man's voice said from somewhere behind the little girl. The gruff tones came from the darkness, beyond the light of the fire.

"Who's there?" Andrew demanded. The little girl didn't say a word or take her eyes off of him as she slowly raised her right hand and pointed her small index finger directly at Andrew.

The man who owned the voice in the darkness stepped forward into the circle of firelight.

He was wearing a red flannel shirt and a weathered blue baseball cap, pulled down almost low enough to cover a pair of exhausted eyes. Not the kind of exhaustion that came from spending a great deal of time on the trail, but the kind that looked more akin to inner torment.

His face was covered in at least a few days' worth of scruff. He raised his own right hand and pointed a pistol directly at Andrew.

"You need to sit back down," the man said as he

cocked back the hammer of his weapon.

"I don't have any money, but you two can have whatever supplies you need. She looks like she needs a doctor!" Andrew stammered as he sat back down on his log.

"This isn't a robbery, and I don't think a doctor can help her now," he said.

Andrew looked from the man pointing a gun, to the little girl still pointing her finger at him, and a wave of recognition and confusion washed across his face

"What is this, then?" Andrew begged.

The man with the gun answered with a question of his own: "You can see her, can't you?"

Andrew looked back at the little girl and screamed in frustration, "Of course I can see her!"

"You've seen her before, haven't you?" asked the man.

Tears began to pour down Andrew's face.

"Yes. I've seen her before," Andrew finally admitted. "A long time ago."

The gruff man responded with a threatening tone, never missing a beat.

"That little girl appeared in my bedroom twenty years ago when I was about her age, and she's been with me everywhere I've been since that day. Every single place that I've gone. She's been there, with those dark, dead eyes, just staring at me. And when I sleep, she usually finds me there, too. I've never known peace. I've never known love. Just me and her. Until right now, no one else has ever seen her."

"Twenty years ago," Andrew repeated with a sigh, looking down at the ground.

"Everyone thought I was crazy," the man with the gun said. "Why wouldn't they? A little boy who sees little girls that no one else can see? I guess that does sound pretty crazy. They tried every medication in the world, but she never went away. When I got a bit older, I decided to just tell everyone I was better. I told them I wasn't seeing things anymore. I told them I was okay, but I never was. She's been my constant companion for twenty fucking years and I want her to go away!"

"Does she talk?" Andrew asked

The man with the gun laughed, "No, she's not much of a conversationalist at all. She mostly just stares. I just got her to start pointing at shit about a year ago."

"What happened a year ago?" Andrew asked.

"About a year ago I decided to pretend that maybe I'm not crazy. I decided to pretend that maybe this little girl that no one else can see really is standing there. I decided to pretend that she wasn't a figment of my insane imagination. Then I decided to try to find out what the hell she wants from me.

"I started doing a little research. Turns out, a little girl named Caroline went missing in a town about a hundred miles from where I grew up, just a few days before this little girl showed up in my bedroom. Caroline was wearing a blue dress the day she went missing.

"She was still wearing that blue dress over a year later when they found her body. The coroner said some really unimaginable things had happened to her before she died, but they never found out who did it. I decided to ask Caroline here—or Caroline's ghost I reckon—who did those things to her.

"That's when she started pointing, and I've been following the end of that little finger up and down the Appalachian Trail for the past several months. I'm about out of resources for this sort of thing. I was about to just give up. But now, here we are, with you sitting on the other end of Coraline's finger, and me wondering why she's pointing at you—and why the fuck you can see her."

"The Lord forgave me for that!" Andrew blurted out defiantly, unable to hide his guilt any longer.

"The Lord can mind his own goddamn business," the man with the gun retorted. "You took Caroline's life and you ruined mine. This here is between the three of us. Don't concern the Lord, far as I can see."

The man looked over at Caroline, who was still pointing at Andrew. Then, without another word, he turned back toward Andrew and pulled the trigger.

The sound of the shot echoed through the dark night as blood began to flow from Andrew's abdomen.

"That there's probably gonna take a little bit to kill ya," the man said. "Don't worry, I'll stick around long enough to make sure you're dead."

Andrew fell to the ground clutching his gut and moaning. The man with the gun looked over at Caroline. She put her pointing hand down at her side and, without acknowledging the man with the gun at all, turned around and walked away into the darkness.

J. WARREN WELCH is a husband, father of daughters, lover of squats and deadlifts, wearer of leggings, commenter on social issues, and writer of prose and poetry who resides in East Tennessee.

STILL

S.S. MARSHALL

In the foothills of the Appalachian Mountains, beyond the dense trees and smoky fog that blankets the landscape, barely stands a moonshine still, forgotten over time by all but one man.

Down a small, winding trail that leads far into the woods, you will find the still, overgrown with moss and worn with time.

The owner was a man by the name of Walter James.

It was 1932—a time when moonshine runs were rampant and dodging the law was the way to make a living.

Walter was very protective of his land, his still, and his recipe. No one knew what went into his brew except him. And when he died, the ingredients died with him.

Walter was a reclusive man who didn't take kindly to trespassers. He only spoke to himself, his still, a small black-and-gray-spotted dog named Pepper, and any clients that he would sell his liquid cash to.

He spent the majority of his life avoiding interaction besides this and focused his attention solely on concocting the perfect ingredients to his mountain dew.

Walter was by no means a young man. His face laid out a pattern of wrinkles running back and forth across his sun-stained skin and his hair—what was left of it—had turned as white as the fog that nestled itself around his feet as he walked gingerly toward his well-worn path to the still.

People in the towns surrounding the mountains had long been aware of Walter James, but they also knew better than to go near his property. Walter knew folks were afraid of him, so he was confident his still would always be safe. He played it out like a well-performed role on the days he did find the need to go into the town for supplies and groceries. He didn't make eye contact nor conversation with anyone. If someone approached him, he would growl or tell them to get away.

He wasn't the nicest man the folk around those parts had encountered; in fact, he was known to many as "The Bear in the Woods" due to his grizzly beard and aggressive temper.

Walter had lost his wife many years before, and buried her under a tree on the land near the still. She was the only one who saw the soft side of the sandpaper exterior he put up to others. When Alice died, so did any attempt at love, happiness or fulfillment—until Walter built his still, which he named after his late wife. Just being able to say her name again, even if it was to a piece of metal, felt familiar and comforting.

He put all his emotion into Alice the still, and that was enough for him.

The clients who asked for his product knew to keep conversation short and time between deliveries long. Walter had been quite the runner in his younger days, but over the years time and solitude had made their homes in his mind, body, and heart. Walter's routine was thoughtless and routine, as each day he went about the normalcy he had come to call his own.

As the leaves gave way to yellow and orange hues on the first day of autumn, he awoke and, as he had every day before, Walter made his coffee from a small brown bag of grounds and cracked two eggs into a large cast iron pan atop a small gas stove.

He set the table for one, per usual, ate his breakfast, grabbed a crate of jars, and headed out to his Alice, with Pepper not far behind him.

He was moving a bit slower today and was finding himself shorter of breath as he continued past a small cross under an oak tree and toward the small shed that was hidden back in the tangled vine-covered cove.

He nodded at Alice with what was a smile in his terms, sat his crate down and began to unload the glass mason jars onto the ground at the foot of the still before pouring some moonshine in a jar to taste the batch.

He'd had nary a drop touch his tongue as he put the jar up to his lips, but he began to lose his vision. The world around him grew blurry, and Walter collapsed to the ground, hitting his head on a nearby rock.

It has never been determined if the heart attack killed him first, or if it was the blow to his head when he careened to the earth. But Walter James had died the way he lived: alone with only his dog and a jar of moonshine in his hand.

Due to his decision to live removed from society, and by placing his still under the same constraints, the body of Walter James was never found, and it decomposed under the canopy of trees and Appalachian rains.

His dog Pepper was loyal to the end and lay by his side until she, too, ultimately succumbed to the elements and hunger. Walter was eighty-three years old. And that's just the beginning of this story...

• • •

Walter's still remained hidden and out of the sight of other humans for decades, which only proved how incredibly smart and careful Walter was when he chose that spot for his Alice.

It wasn't until exactly fifty years later, in the summer of 1982, that Walter's secret was exposed to the world, along with his restless soul.

As the want for fresh produce gained popularity within restaurants, more and more families found themselves out in nature, scouring for wild mushrooms and roots. One such family was the Wolfe family of southern Virginia. Five family members—Geneva, Jean, Michael, Lee and Elizabeth—spread out into the forest in search of what folks called chicken of the woods mushrooms. They grew at the base of trees and could be hard to find. But when you did, you were in for a large gathering, as these mushrooms grew in bunches.

Two of the family members, Michael and Elizabeth, wandered further into the matrix of trees before coming upon a small wooden cabin in the middle of what used to be a clearing. The place was run down, as was indicated by the lack of shingles on the roof, the exterior dominated by twisted green vines, and the dilapidated porch that once held two white rocking chairs. You could barely tell that it used to be a habitable dwelling.

Michael and Elizabeth decided not to inspect, and instead continued past, looking left and right for the orange bunches at the base of the trees as they advanced.

Michael stopped a spell to tie his shoe as Elizabeth went on ahead. A moment later, the peaceful rustling of the leaves was broken by a shrill scream of terror. Against his better judgment, Michael ran to find his sister and found her running toward him out of a patch of brush. Between what breaths she had left, she gasped her words as she exclaimed she had seen bones lying next to what looked like a large silver pot.

Michael, always the skeptic and professed realist, thought her ridiculous and having wild imaginings, and went to see for himself. He strolled gallantly up to the covering of bush, pushed through the thickets, and disappeared among them.

He stood in the darkness, trying to look around. As he began stumbling about, he kicked something hard and heard a clinking sound. He bent over and picked up a weathered jar covered in dirt.

At that moment, a stream of light infiltrated the hideaway and illuminated a rusted object. There before Michael was what Elizabeth had been talking about. He wiped the tarnish off the side and stared at his muddled reflection in a silver moonshine still. It was then he heard a noise behind him, like someone was creeping up. Thinking it was Elizabeth coming to check on him and tell him she told him so, he wheeled around.

A few seconds later, a blood-curdling scream arose from within the foreboding cove, echoing for miles off the mountains. And then—

Silence.

Elizabeth, struck with terror, called out for Michael, her voice a nervous tremble, but to no avail.

Thinking he might be waiting to scare her, she began yelling out for him to come out. But he never did.

After what seemed like hours, though it had only been a few moments in reality, Elizabeth took off running and screaming the names of other members of her family, looking back to see if anyone was behind her. No one was, that she could see at least. And then, as she turned to look ahead, there was the silhouette of someone in her path. His eyes were sunken in and his overalls tattered. The foggy air swirled around his feet and encase his body. Ever so slowly he stepped toward her, his limp causing him to sway side to side.

His movements were unsteady, adding to the already terrifying aspects of the encounter. The figure moved in and out of the fog and trees as if he were playing a game of hide and seek, every time it seemed you knew his next move, you were transported to a new place where there was still no escape. There was only one image of him, but the air containing him had her surrounded. The closer he moved, she matched him step for step backing away in the opposite direction. Below him developed another form of a small transparent animal with eyes glowing like ruby gems glistening in the moonlight, a phantom sidekick that followed its owner, even in death. She squinted her eyes to adjust to the fog and through the mist walked a black and white dog, frothy at the mouth, ambling beat for beat with the pace its owner had set on their course toward Elizabeth.

As he continued his line, for a moment his face was flooded with cascading light from the treed overhead. The brightness revealed a skeleton of a man only mere feet from her, one of what once was human and containing eyes of white as if they were permanently rolled back in his head, yet glowing with a blinding intensity in which Elizabeth had never seen. The sight nearly immobilized her, but she quickly turned to run. Not even one more step was taken. She let out a lasting scream before there was again, silence.

A calm fell over the area where they stood not even moments ago. Not a breath of air, not a breath of life. Silence enveloped the area. The trees now held their own secrets of what they witnessed. Michael and Elizabeth had seen the still and Walter had seen them. It was that moment they found that moonshiners protect their proof, even in death.

]As the sun set behind the trees, the remaining three family members picked up their baskets of mushrooms they had forged and yelled for the other two that had drifted far into the tree line. Thinking they were playing around, Jean grew angry at the fact they hadn't returned yet. Lee too felt the aggravation as he wiped sweat from his head and looked down at his watch. If Michael and Elizabeth come back empty handed, there would be hell to pay.

Geneva, who was the rational one of the group left, suggested they start looking for them instead of waiting around much longer against the rose colored sky that was on full display at sunset. As they began their journey weaving in and out of the trees, they began seeing what looked like another form darting in and out of the shadows around them. Thinking it was only their imagination, they chose to pay little attention. Breaking the silence immediately, the sound of a bark echoed through the area. The three turned every which way trying to find where it came from, however their efforts were to no avail.

Since it was getting dark, they decided to stay together to go find the last two. They walked for what seemed like miles shouting the duo's names and growing more and more worried with each passing shadow of the impending nightfall. As much as they didn't want to, they knew they needed to split up.

Luckily, Lee had thought to bring walkie talkies so they could correspond with each other for just this purpose. Unfortunately, Michael and Elizabeth didn't take one before they excursion. Lee knew these woods like the back of his hand, so he chose to go off on his own. Geneva and Jean approved of his choice, took the other walkie talkie, and headed off in the opposite direction.

They came to the agreement that if no one had seen Elizabeth or Michael in half an hour, to radio and meet right back where they split up. Jean was wearing a bandanna, so they used that to tie around a tree for reference. The light was receding fast, so they all knew it was a race against the sun.

Before too long, Jean and Geneva came upon a cabin that appeared out of what seemed like thin air. Ironically, not wanting to become the main characters of a horror film, they pushed on along a covered trail. Still yelling the names into the hazy orange light and receiving no response. The cracking of branches startled them each time one was found under their feet. Forward they pressed on their determined path, holding close to each other for assurance. Suddenly, Jean stopped dead in place and spun around aiming her flashlight beam frantically from ground to sky. "Did you hear that? It was a growl!" Jean whispered nervously. Geneva's flashlight joined Jean's in the search though she replied, "I didn't hear anything. Where was it coming from?" Just then a black mass burst through the brush in front of them and ran back toward the old cabin. The force of the rush pushed both girls to the cold ground. As the scrambled back to their feet, they saw a light flickering off of a tree close to the spot of the cabin. Without thinking, they took off full speed further into the woods.

On the other side of the path, Lee struggled with direction. He usually was good at figuring out trails, but with the darkness falling, he was losing sight of where his location was. With each step he grew angrier with Elizabeth and Michael and swore he would make them regret ever leaving the group. As he continued his carefully navigated line, he began to fee very uneasy, as if someone was watching his every step. He stopped momentarily to smack his flashlight a few times as it was getting dim. As he stood still, he heard the words, "Go. Now!" fill his ear as if someone was standing inside his head shouting them. He turned around and found nothing but his own footprints in the soft mud behind him with the faint light emitting from his flashlight. He smacked it one more time, harder than any other time, and a strong light came out of the top. He used this second wind to sprint away from the voice that would end up haunting him infinitely.

Half an hour passed with neither team finding Michael or Elizabeth. Jean picked up the walkie talkie and radioed Lee. They weren't as far from each other as they thought, so they reconvened at the original tree they left. Each person expressed the horror they felt in those woods and couldn't imagine being lost as long as Elizabeth and Michael had. They all came to the conclusion, they had to keep going and find them. Daylight was almost gone and so was their patience.

The trio trekked further into the mountains. In front of them, they saw a dead end. It looked to be a impossible mass of bush with no visibility to the other side. Geneva decided to hang back while Lee and Jean slowly inched forward. With no warning, something stopped them all in their tracks. They heard what sounded like Michael's voice telling them, "Don't dare to come any closer!"

"Stop playing and get out of there!" Lee scolded loudly.

The response was the voice of Elizabeth saying, "We

can't. But you can come in".

Entirely over this whole situation, Lee began toward the voices before he physically could not put one more foot in front of the other. Jean and Geneva could no longer move either. It was as if a heavy weight had lowered itself onto their shoulders, pressing down on them rendering them unable to take another step.

Ahead, the leaves and branches rustled with no explanation. Fearing a wild animal, they fought with all their might to break the grasp of whatever was pressing down on them. Suddenly, out of the rustling brush, something rushed not only at them, but through them.

They stood as stone while they were bombarded repeatedly by a mass of darkness and chilled air. They couldn't scream. They couldn't move. They stood mouths agape praying for this entity to leave them alone. A figure emerged from within the mass, eyes burning with the light of a thousand stars. Jean, Geneva and Lee threw their arms up in front of their faces to shield their eyes from the blaze of fluorescent glare.

Finally, Lee escaped Walter's grip and grabbed the other two. They ran faster than they thought humanly possible out of those woods, forgetting the other two and leaving them to chance. No matter how far they found themselves out of the woods, they never could shake the feeling that someone was chasing them.

Faster.

Constantly.

• • •

Yes, those three of the five members made it back out of the woods, however, all three were institutionalized shortly after their return home.

Due to their increasing fear of a phantom person following them and entering their thoughts and dreams, the members of the Wolfe family found it nearly impossible to deal with the after effects of what they saw. Physically, all three had irreversible damaging effects to their eyes from the sharp lights they were drowned in that evening in 1983.

Despite ongoing efforts of doctors to bring out information, the three refused to speak, and if they tried, it came out in screams in the middle of the night. Against everything they wanted to do, the Wolfe family decided to send Lee, Geneva and Jean to a mental institution for their own safety.

The doctors assigned to aide in the recovery of the Wolfe family's case, found themselves struggling with her own sanity at times.

Doctor Louise Gilreath and Doctor Heath Grayson conducted many sessions in the course of 8 years at the facility with each of the three members on different occasions. Within these sessions, the patients would see things that weren't there, tell them to run and randomly begin screaming and hiding their eyes. With the assistance of another Doctor at the institution, Doctor

Bennett Terry, they split their time attacking the unseen and unspoken issue from every angle imaginable.

Eventually, after hospital management agreed to the session, the three were able to sit in one room with Doctor Russell and Doctor Louise and recount that evening in 1983. It took seven hours of episodes and digging, but they finally allowed the doctors into their mind and their past with Walter James.

It didn't take long to realize that neither doctor wanted to believe such a far fetched tale, but as lifelong residents of the Appalachian region, they found the stories of Walter James, his temper and his mysterious disappearance from being seen around the town again so many years ago, more likely to be believed.

Just as no one ever found the body of Walter James until Michael and Elizabeth discovered it in 1983, their two bodies were never discovered either. It was like they never existed and vanished without a trace. Not one iota of evidence or cause.

That same night after the Wolfe family opened up about their horrific experiences within the woods, exactly 10 years to the day after the incident, Jean was found dead in her room after gouging her eyes out with a piece of glass she found in her room.

Not even 24 hours after her death, Lee's body was found hanging from the bars of the windows in his room and shortly after, Geneva jumped to hear demise from a small balcony on the 5th floor of the hospital.

It was if they had been punished for their admittance

to what had occurred. In a way, it was if Walter James had killed them from beyond the grave, finishing the job he had started years ago. Those five family members that made their way onto his land that night had trespassed. They had found his secret and his wrath for doing so.

Since they were the only ones that knew where his still Alice stood, they must be made quiet. The lingering effects to their eyes from the lights that evening made it impossible for them to find their way back to the still even if they wanted to, which was Walter's plan all along. In the end, his revenge was foolproof.

Since the deaths of the Wolfe family members, many have followed their footsteps into the foothills into unspeakable events. Not all were able to make their way through the winding and confusing paths of the trees, however, those that dared to go past the "No Trespassing" signs, found themselves more than they bargained for.

The still was removed mere weeks after the confessions and deaths of the Wolfe family, but Alice wasn't what these seekers were searching for. They wanted to find Walter James and stand toe to toe with his presence and story. Though the still was gone, his spirit stayed to protect his land and his home. In fact, they say the removal of the still angered him even more so, making the risk going onto his property more dangerous than it ever was before.

Yet, people still muster the courage, or stupidity, to

venture into the vast woods into the unknown happenings of what may lie ahead. Those that make it that far, never make it back out. They validate the stories of the Wolfe family that came before them. They find that these aren't just ghost stories in a book, they are real and they are ongoing.

Of the ones that went in and made it out, none were ever the same. They slowly went insane and ended up in the institution, either living out their remaining days there or ending their days their by their own hand. So in reality, no one that trespasses on the land of Walter James makes it out alive.

If you ever find yourself in the Appalachian area, this is your warning, and I suggest you take heed. If not, you may find yourself lost, with only the light of two eyes to see the way and your mind in a jar on a shelf of a distillery. You don't have to take my word for it, but don't take a chance either.

You may find yourself in the midst of Walter James and his little dog Pepper. Hey, you don't have to believe me, but he exists.

I swear.

With certainty of 150 proof.

S. S. MARSHALL has spilled words across the writing spectrum. From newspapers, to magazines, to anthologies, to speeches and blogs; she puts ink to her thoughts. Born and raised in the foothills of East Tennessee, Marshall came back to Tennessee and her roots by way of Orlando, Florida, after working as an entertainment lead and trainer at Universal Studios. Marshall views every day as an adventure and every experience as a story.

LIGHT

DUSTIN STREET

The Light started following Daddy home when he was sixteen, and it never stopped.

He told the family all about it one night as he rolled in from porch pickin' over at Harlan's, across the Gap. He was a bit lit up at the time, from what he called Harlan's "special juice," which he said was just like the grape juice the kids drank in their lunches. But Kate, his eldest daughter, had just turned sixteen, and she knew all about "special juice," so he wasn't fooling anyone.

It was Ann, Kate's little sister, who sparked the conversation in the first place. She was only nine, but she had a keen eye and an insatiable curiosity, and she had noticed that her daddy always seemed a little bit distracted for the first few minutes whenever he would get home late at night. She'd watch him come to the front door and stop just short, always hesitating, checking over his shoulder, as if he expected someone else to be there.

"Why do you do that, Daddy? Stay outside so long," Ann had asked him. "Are you waiting for someone?"

"No, honey, it's the Light," he said, his expression shifting from a moment of concern to warm adoration for his daughter. "The one that follows me home every night. I always like to watch it leave before I come inside."

Sarah, their momma, was none too amused. She wasn't the typical "holler wife" who minded her husband having a good time with his friends, playing music and singing and shooting the breeze until the late hours. But the drinking had been getting worse this week in particular, and she always made it clear that she didn't want Daddy filling the girls' minds with nonsense—strong drink clouding his mind or not.

"There ain't no light, Bill, my *goodness*," she said, making a funny face at the girls behind their daddy's back as she embraced him. "Don't scare Ann with any more of your ghost stories."

"I'm not scared, Momma," Ann said, but Kate was quick to grab her by the ponytail, jerking lightly at the younger girl's frizzy brown hair.

"You're scared of everything, Ann," Kate said. "It hasn't even been a week since the last time you wet the bed after a nightmare."

Ann's face morphed into a tortured grimace at having her hair pulled, not to mention her embarrassment at Kate's revelation.

"You hush up, Katie! It was an accident!" Ann cried, trying desperately to escape her sister's grasp on her locks so that she could turn around and nail her in the gut. "You're one to talk! You been having bad dreams lately, too! And don't act like it ain't true!"

It was true, in fact. But Kate didn't much want to be reminded of the inky, dark water that had been haunting her dreams of late, so she gave another hard yank. Ann squealed from having her hail pulled, and Momma intervened with her usual chorus about how sensitive Ann's scalp was.

"Hey now," their father said, ramming into the kitchen counter as he stumbled over to them to break up their quarrel. He pointed a finger at Kate, a half-smile on his lips as the words came out. It was the kind of smile that let Kate know there was a lot on Daddy's mind. He dove a hand into his jean pocket as he approached, pulling out a small, flat object cut in the shape of a triangle. A guitar pick, Kate realized.

"You be nice to your sister. You have to look out for her, you hear?" Daddy warned, flashing a momentary dark glance at his eldest girl. "This guitar pick was given to me by my best buddy Arnold, many years ago. He was like a brother to me, and in some ways I think he's still taking care of me to this day."

Kate took the pick from her father and smiled. "Thanks, Daddy. I'll hold on to it," she said.

"Hold on to your sister, too," he said, gesturing his finger over to Ann. "Always protect her, no matter what."

The girls separated, a mischievous grin painted on Kate's face as she mockingly patted Ann's mussed hair and said, "Yes, Daddy."

Ann crossed her arms in a huff, her lips in a full pout. Kate could tell she was mad because Daddy didn't give *her* a guitar pick, too. Especially because she thought she was the favorite.

"And besides," Daddy said, looking over at their mother, "the Light ain't no ghost. It's my guardian angel."

Kate watched as Ann's face lit up at the idea, although she herself wasn't as sold on it. Though she believed in God, and thought angels probably were real, she didn't think they had the time to walk among the living and watch their every move.

"Like the ones Miss Jill told us about in Sunday School?"

"That's right," Daddy said, bending down to bring his face level with his youngest daughter's. "The Light has been around since I was about Kate's age. And on really dark nights when Daddy's scared, it follows me home and makes sure I'm all right."

Ann beamed as Daddy tapped her nose with his index finger. Kate could tell her father really believed it, too; there was something about his look. He seemed so confident. But there was something else in his eyes—a lingering heaviness in them she couldn't put her finger on.

"I want a guardian angel, too," Ann said. "For my bad dreams."

Daddy stood back to his full height and drew Ann in for a hug, reaching over and pulling Kate in as well. "I bet you've got one, you just can't see it. It's probably looking out for you when you don't even realize it."

Ann grinned again and ran over to the front door. She opened it up and gazed out beyond the screen of the storm door, into the darkness, and said, "Good night, guardian angel, wherever you are."

Kate rolled her eyes, turning over the smooth wax guitar pick in her fingers, appreciating the slick texture of it, the way it felt warm and familiar in her hands.

"Well, if you don't quit drinking so much of Harlan's homemade wine, your guardian angel's going to be working overtime," Momma said. "Now say your good-nights and get off to bed. Ann? You too."

"Yes, Momma," Ann replied obediently as she bolt-ed back over to Daddy, who scooped her up in a giant embrace.

"Sweet dreams, girls," he said, patting Ann on the back and throwing Kate a wink.

A few moments later, Kate watched as Daddy stum-bled into the hallway, with Momma not far behind. As she went to follow them, she turned to see that Ann had returned to the front door.

"Come on," Kate said. "Time for bed."

Ann either didn't hear her or wasn't listening, because she stood there, perplexed, as if she could see something outside.

"Ann!" Kate shouted, and finally, the younger sister turned around.

"Okay!" Ann shouted defiantly, and then she stomped past Kate with a huff, and marched toward the hallway that led to their rooms without another word.

Kate rolled her eyes again and turned on her heel to follow Ann. A few steps away from the threshold into the hallway, though, Kate couldn't help herself. She, too, turned back to look toward the front door, wondering with curiosity what Ann might have been looking at.

Seeing nothing but the darkness outside, Kate closed the door and secured the latch in place. After checking it again—because locking doors was just something she always did, and did again—Kate switched off the kitchen light and stepped into the hallway. Her room was the last door on the left, right next to the bathroom they all shared.

As she approached, she heard water running, and the sound of her father's voice, low and anxious. It sounded as though he were speaking to someone in hushed tones he didn't want anyone else to hear. Kate paused just outside the bathroom door and listened. She could finally make out what he was saying.

"Where is it? Where are you? Where is it? Where are you?"

He splashed water in his face, keeping his head bent over the sink, and repeating the words over and over again.

"Where is it? Where are you? Where is it…"

Kate stood perplexed in the hallway, turning to see if

Momma was anywhere in sight. Their bedroom light was on, so she must have been turning down the covers.

When Kate turned back to her father, she crossed the threshold into the bathroom and laid a hand on his shoulder. He didn't jump or startle, but he did suddenly stop muttering to himself.

With a slow, deep breath, Daddy raised his head to look into the large, round mirror above the sink. His eyes met Kate's in the reflection, all traces of the funny, happy man his family knew banished from his features.

"Katie," he whispered breathlessly. He hadn't called her that in years. Not since she had told him she preferred the more grown-up-sounding *Kate* instead.

"Daddy, what's wrong?" Kate inquired, her voice trembling at the disheveled sight of her father's behavior.

"It's gone, Katie," he said, still keeping his voice to a low whisper. His eyes were ringed by angry red circles. It looked as though he had been rubbing them.

"What is?" Katie asked. "What's gone?"

"The Light," he breathed, and tears streamed from both his eyes. "It didn't follow me home tonight."

• • •

T he giant cistern sat in the midst of the clearing, in just the same place it had been last time. It was surrounded on three sides by dark forest, and on the other, a ramshackle cabin *with golden light spewing from within.*

The dark water inside the wooden container was mostly still, almost calming. Kate could see the reflection of her pale, round face and straight, shoulder-length brown hair. The water was quiet, aside from the light sloshes of tiny waves smacking against the wooden frame of the cauldron.

Kate was suddenly aware of someone humming nearby. The sound was entrancing, like a hypnotic drone, and she could feel herself growing uncomfortable the longer she stood listening to it.

Discomfort compounded into unease; she felt a gurgle in her stomach. Kate hugged her tummy with trembling arms, and suddenly felt ice-cold all over. The humming grew louder and louder, and the water beneath her began to toss and roil.

Kate noticed a faint glow coming from the bottom of the giant wooden tub, illuminating the dark water. Small, black, lumpy shapes with fibrous tendrils all around them—which Kate could not recall having seen before—swam in its depths.

"Oh!" Kate screamed, as a searing pain erupted in her gut. Kate heaved, moving her hands to grip the wooden sides of the giant cistern. Her body doubled over on its own, forcing her face down closer to the dark water. She took in a breath, trying to steady herself, and was met with an acrid stench that reminded her of rotten fruit mixed with pine sap.

"Oh, God," Kate said, feeling the bile and contents of her stomach rising beyond her control. The humming was loud in her ears now, and she could hear clapping and stomping all around her.

She turned her head to the side, trying to orient herself, and was surprised to see Ann standing next to her. The humming had been coming from her.

"Ann?" Kate heard her scratchy voice croak. But Ann didn't answer. She just kept humming.

At last, Kate couldn't keep it down any longer. She turned back to the water inside the cistern, opened her mouth, and let the vomit spew forth like an endless fountain, with tiny little pieces of something springing from her mouth. She felt them coming up her throat, crowding each other trying to get through, and scratching the lining of her esophagus. The burn was so intense, she thought she might suffocate.

For a precious moment, Kate was able to stop puking long enough to see what it was that was coming out of her. As she peered down into the water, which had now turned a vibrant azure in the intense light that came from the depths of the cauldron, she could just make out what appeared to be hundreds of small, smooth triangles.

Guitar picks.

They swam in the bright-blue radiance, accompanied by sick and whatever the fibrous things in the water were. Kate could feel a scream building in her chest, but before she could let it go, something grasped the back of her head and pushed her face down into the depths...

• • •

Kate woke with a start, mercifully back in her own bedroom. In a flurry, she let her hands roam over her face, her torso and stomach. She was dry, and she certainly didn't feel as though she had just thrown up her insides by the gallon.

And thankfully, she didn't think her stomach was full of guitar picks, like the one her father had given her earlier.

It had only been a dream. The same dream she'd had so many times before. The one with the big cistern—a word she'd had to look up at the library when she couldn't think of one she knew to describe the giant vat of dark water.

This time, though, the dream had been different. This time, Ann had been there. And Kate had never vomited into the water before tonight—much less hurled up dozens of guitar picks.

Just my mind, Kate thought. *Daddy gave me a guitar pick and my mind put it in the dream. Ann was jealous and she was in it, too. That's all.*

Kate had always prided herself on her healthy levels of skepticism. Where the rest of her family always fell over themselves for some supernatural or religious explanation of the events that shaped their daily lives, Kate liked to think that good things and bad things just happened by chance. Luck of the draw. God didn't have time to sit around and decide the fates of millions and millions of people based on their actions.

She sat up in her bed and rubbed her eyes, glancing up at the clock on her wall to see what time it was—half-past three in the morning. The big numbers on the old clock face were lit up in a brilliant blue hue. But—

That's odd, she thought. *The moon can't be that bright.*

As she pondered the curious light, she turned her head

to the high window at the far side of her room and saw exactly where it had come from.

A glowing sphere—an orb, floating just outside her window. Its edges were undefined, and nebulous tendrils circled around it like the corona she had learned surrounded the Sun in her science classes. Kate sat transfixed by the hovering light, her stomach in tense knots, as the orb seemed to be waiting for something— staring at her, seeking her acknowledgment.

She was only vaguely aware of the rush of footsteps in the hallway outside her bedroom door, and as they grew closer, the ball of light backed away from her window in a flit of motion that was almost too quick for Kate to register.

"Wait—" she said, jumping up from her bed and crossing the floor to the window. But by the time she got there, the light had zoomed away, a blur of luminance disappearing into the lightless night.

CRASH.

The door to Kate's room slammed open, hitting her wall with a force that shook her to her core. She whipped around to see Daddy stumbling into her darkened room. Her eyes had adjusted enough to see the wild, frantic look on his face. His skin had gone pale and was clammy with a sheen of sweat.

"Let's go!" he shouted, his breath coming in heaves. "Get in the basement. Now!"

"Daddy?"

"Kate, honey, we need to move!" Daddy seemed to

have sobered up in spite of his manic behavior. His voice was austere, demanding. She had never see him like this before. *Afraid* was not a word she had ever associated with him.

Before she could think another thought, Kate's legs carried her across the floor and to the doorway. With a furtive glance back at her window, Kate saw only darkness outside—no sign of the mysterious light—and she followed her father out into the hall. They moved quickly toward the basement stairwell, where Momma and Ann were waiting.

Momma appeared confused—frustrated, even. She was massaging her temples with slender fingers, her eyes closed and her mouth drawn into a taut line.

Ann clutched her teddy tightly, looking terrified.

Once Kate, her sister, and mother were all safely down the basement steps, they watched in silence as Daddy placed a heavy wooden plank across the door leading back into the house. The plank settled into the steel hooks mounted on either side of the door frame.

"Daddy, what's happening?" Ann whined. Her legs were trembling and her big brown eyes were wide with fear. Their father descended the steps and sprinted across the floor, heading up toward the cellar door, where he secured another heavy beam to prevent the door from being opened from the outside.

"Daddy!" Kate called, echoing her sister; she wanted some explanation as well.

Daddy didn't respond; he pulled a flashlight off the

dusty shelf next to the stairs and handed it to Momma. Out of breath and frantic, he made his way over to the canning table and opened the case on top. From within, he pulled out his 12-gauge and beckoned the family to the dark corner at the far end of the house, where an old couch sat moth-eaten and worn.

"Come sit," he said, his face still wild and exasperated as he began pushing shells into the gun's loading flap.

"Bill, what in *God's name* is going on?" Momma demanded, a mix of fear and consternation waxing hot behind her tired green eyes.

"Shhh," Daddy said, putting a finger to his lips, silencing them so that the only sounds were Ann's heavy breathing and Momma clicking her tongue. Kate watched as Daddy moved his index finger from his lips to his ear, as if beckoning them to listen in the dark silence.

Then he pointed upward, to the ceiling above them, where the kitchen sat.

Kate didn't hear it at first, but as her ears adjusted to the quiet, and filtered out the noise in her immediate surroundings, she could hear a *tap-tap-tap* coming from above them. Faint at first, the rapping grew more incessant, and Kate realized something was knocking against their storm door.

"Daddy, who is that? Is someone here?" Kate asked in a hushed whisper, but Daddy swatted his hand at her and shushed her quiet again.

The tapping let up, and for a moment, all was quiet

again. And then—

BANG.

A thunderous explosion from upstairs, the unmistakable sound of shattering glass, and the heavy plopping sound of something hitting the kitchen floor, followed by violent scratching noises.

The front door, Kate realized. *Someone had just kicked down the front door.*

Both Momma and Ann let out screams, and Kate gasped in terror as she latched onto her father's arm.

With his free hand, Daddy cupped his fingers over Ann's mouth and went back to shushing Momma again.

"Quiet!" he hissed. "Everybody *quiet!*"

Seconds passed, but every moment stretched on for what felt like a lifetime to Kate. She tried to focus on something—anything—other than the raw fear that ran the length of her body as her family sat huddled together on the ragged couch in the quiet darkness. She shifted her eyes down to her feet, which were dimly illuminated by Momma's flashlight. Her toes had dug into the dirt floor of the basement, seeking purchase in her terror, and the dusty black stuff was now caked beneath her toenails.

"Bill—" Momma whimpered, but before she could utter another word, they heard a *pitter-patter*ing noise above them. It sounded almost like a dog walking along the hardwood floors, but the footfalls were much heavier.

A bear? Kate wondered. It was the only thing she could think of that might make footsteps that loud.

The steps echoed above them and began to move from

the kitchen over to the living room, and from the living room to the hallway that led to their bedrooms. The loud scratching noises returned, setting Kate's teeth on edge and forcing her to cup her hands over her ears.

Another crash, followed by more shattering glass, this time on the far end of the house, closest to Ann's room. *Momma's curio cabinet*, Kate realized.

Ann whimpered again, muttering "Daddy, Daddy, *Daddy...*" over and over, rocking back and forth in their father's arms. This time, he didn't urge her to be silent, so Kate turned to her and put a finger to her lips.

"Shhh," Kate whispered, and suddenly, the footsteps grew louder as they returned to the kitchen. There was another crash as whatever creature had broken into their house seemed to collide with something directly above them.

Momma shone the flashlight up to the ceiling as the footsteps resumed. They seemed to make their way back outside the house, leaving the family in silence down in the basement once again.

For a long moment, the quiet seemed to stretch out before them in the damp space of the basement. Kate could hear her heart pounding in her chest and heard the wheezing breaths of—not Ann, as she had thought, but of her father. As she turned in the crook of his arm to get a look at him, Momma shone the light on his face.

Daddy was pale as a ghost, his lips chapped, arid as desert sand. He was covered in a cold sweat and his eyes were closed tightly, as if he were fighting off pain. His chest rose and fell in rapid beats, and the air coming from his nose and mouth made a whistling sound that grew more intense with each passing moment.

"Daddy?" Kate said, placing her hand on his chest to rouse him. "Daddy are you all right?"

Without warning, Daddy sat bolt upright and took in a gasping breath, his eyes wide and wild. And then, another sound joined in with Daddy's gasp. A horrible, shrill screeching cry from upstairs, outside the house. It was like nothing Kate had ever heard in the hollow before—and she had heard just about every animal that lived in these woods over the course of her sixteen years.

The screeching lasted for several moments, finally dying off and fading into the night. When it stopped, Daddy fell back against the couch cushions, his strength drained from him, and his breathing a bit more stable—though still labored.

"Momma!" Ann shouted. "What was that?"

"I don't know, baby," came Momma's trembling voice. She sounded as terrified as Kate felt, all the way down to her bones.

"Bill? Bill!" Momma called to her husband, shaking him with her free hand.

But Daddy was out like a light. He either couldn't hear or couldn't answer back, and the paralyzing fear that had gripped Kate when she heard the screeching gave way to worry about what had come over Daddy in a matter of hours. He'd seemed fine earlier, when he had arrived home from Harlan's. A bit drunk, of course, but that was no different than any other night.

And then Kate remembered the bathroom. She remembered seeing Daddy hovered over the sink, the deep red circles around his eyes, the tears.

"It didn't follow me home tonight," he'd said, talking about the mysterious Light Ann had been so fascinated by.

As Kate turned the words over in her mind, their Momma began to cry. It wasn't like her to do that; Momma was the strong one of the family—the one who held everyone together. The one who dried the girls' tears. But now, it was clear that Momma was at a loss. She drew Ann close to her, embracing the young girl, who in turn embraced her teddy even tighter than she had before.

Kate looked at Daddy again, watched as his chest rose and fell. He appeared to be sleeping, but it was anything but peaceful. Kate could see torment behind his closed eyelids, and she wondered what he might be dreaming about. She wondered what had broken into their house, and why it hadn't thought to come for them in the basement. She wondered what it could have been looking for.

So many questions, and no real way to answer them. She was trapped in their locked basement, on a threadbare old couch, with a dirt floor. Her family was terrified. *Kate* was terrified.

"Besides," Daddy had said in the kitchen earlier, *"the Light ain't no ghost. It's my guardian angel."*

The Light.

Kate thought about the nebulous, glowing orb outside her window. She had seen it just before Daddy had burst into her room and hustled them down into the basement.

Surely it can't be, she thought to herself. She didn't believe in guardian angels and magic lights or any such nonsense. At least, she didn't *think* she believed it.

But Daddy had said it, clear as day.

"It's gone, Katie. The Light. It didn't follow me home tonight."

But Kate was beginning to think that maybe something else *had* followed him home. Something that didn't bode well for Daddy—that didn't bode well for any of them.

Kate must have turned the questions and thoughts and theories over in her mind for a good hour before she realized that Ann and Momma had drifted to sleep. They didn't exactly look comfortable, and nor did Daddy, but Kate accepted the fact that they weren't going back upstairs until daylight. She found herself thankful for that fact, and leaned back into the couch, grabbing a whiff of mothballs and mildew.

Kate leaned against Daddy's chest, listening to his unsteady breathing. The wheezy, whistling sound was still there, and he was still sweating through his clothes. Something was wrong, that much was sure. Daddy was ill, and the strange events that had led them to take shelter downstairs were none too simple to explain.

Eventually, Kate's body forced her into a troubled sleep, where she returned again to the sinister cistern in the forest clearing—and to vomiting up guitar picks, to her sister's terrified face—and to the water, glowing blue and radiant around her face, yet still pitch-dark beneath her. And a new image—a shadow. No, a silhouette. Framed by the doorway to the old shack, and back-lit by the golden glow of lamplight from within.

It was the shape of a woman—but she was shrouded, no light hitting her face so that Kate could identify her.

The last thing Kate remembered seeing when she turned back to the inky blackness of the water was the outline of a pale, white face slowly rising toward her from the abyss. It had sunken, black sockets for eyes, and a wide, gaping maw that opened soundlessly as it grew nearer. Her body went numb as she saw pale, gangly arms with long, white claws attached to the ends, coming up to grab her—to pull her into the depths.

• • •

T he next morning, Kate woke up to Momma shaking her and calling her name. For a moment, before she came to her senses, Kate thought she was back in her own bed, in her own room, and that she had only dreamed the terrifying ordeal that had occurred the night before.

But the damp, moldy smell of the basement wafted past her nose, and she realized that it had all been real.

"Where's Daddy?" Kate said, noticing that the couch was now empty except for her.

"I called Dr. Jones first thing this morning, and he came and helped me get Daddy into bed upstairs," Momma said, idly moving a string of hair out of Kate's eyes. "Are you all right?"

"Is he sick?" Kate asked, sitting upright and suddenly wide awake. She couldn't believe she had slept at all, never mind sleeping through Daddy being moved.

"Yes," Momma said. "He's very, very sick, sweet pea. We're going to have to watch after him for a few days while they try to figure out what's wrong. They're going to have to run some tests. They said we need to keep his symptoms as light as we can."

"I want to see him," Kate said.

"Ann's up there now. She hasn't left his side. I'm sure he'd like to have you for company, too."

Grimacing at the thought that Daddy knew Ann was with him, but not his elder daughter, Kate rose from the couch, her bare feet frigid and filthy against the damp dirt of the basement floor. Before she could take a step, Momma latched onto her arm. Kate turned just in time to watch a shimmering tear escape Momma's eye.

"The house is—" she started, but she couldn't find the words. "Just prepare yourself, Kate. It's bad."

Kate eyed her mother a moment, suddenly unsure whether or not she wished to ascend the stairs. Part of her wanted nothing more than to just crawl back onto the couch and try to return to sleep; maybe she could wake up and have it all be behind her, like the whole thing was some terrible nightmare. But she knew she couldn't let

Daddy think she didn't care about him. She had to go check on him.

Kate's legs trembled as she opened the basement door, and her breath caught in her throat as the hallway beyond came into focus. Deep, jagged grooves carved into the paneled wall ran the length of the corridor, down to the kitchen. She angled her head down and noticed a line of scuff marks all along the wooden floor.

The scratching noises they'd heard last night echoed in Kate's mind; she closed her eyes, and for a moment, she was back in the cold, drafty basement, huddled and scared with her family on the ratty old couch.

Momma shifted past her, patting Kate's shoulder lovingly and exhaling softly as she grabbed a broom that had been propped up against the wall. Kate turned just in time to see Momma sweeping up the shattered pieces of china that had been thrown from her curio cabinet—the cabinet was now missing from the wall at the end of the hall outside her bedroom, Kate noticed.

"Momma…"

Momma glanced at Kate for the briefest of moments, but kept to her work, saying only, "It's fine, sweet pea. You should go see your daddy."

The sound of the shattered glass shards scooting over the floor echoed down the hallways as Momma swept up the mess. Kate shuffled wordlessly down the corridor toward Momma and Daddy's bedroom, dreading what she might see when she rounded the corner of the door frame. Would Daddy *look* sick? Would he seem like himself at all? Maybe he had improved since this morning.

She heard Daddy's voice before she saw him. He sounded faint, his words coming out in short, breathy whimpers.

When Kate stepped into the room, she saw him lying there in his bed, drenched in sweat, and clinging to Ann's hand. Ann looked as though she were trying her best not to cry, but Kate could see the reflective sheen of tears pooling in her eyes.

"...*Light...gone...back at the Gap...she has it...don't go... the Gap...she has it...she has it...don't go...Light...it's gone...*"

Daddy's words were disjointed, muddled. Sometimes he'd repeat the same word or phrase twice, sometimes he'd say them out of order. Kate couldn't make sense of what he was saying as she took a seat on the other side of the bed from him and grasped his free hand.

"Daddy," Kate said, "we're here. We're here for you. Do you need anything?"

"...*the Light...back at the Gap...the Gap...don't go...she has it...she has it...*"

"I'm scared, Kate," Ann said, releasing the dammed-up tears from her eyes, letting them cascade freely down her cheeks.

"Me too," Kate said, tightening her grip on Daddy's hand.

"We have to do something," Ann choked out between sobs. "We have to get Daddy's Light back."

Kate looked away from her father then, and met Ann's

gaze. Her younger sister was looking at her as if she expected Kate to have the final say—some hidden wisdom that she should be able to call upon in Daddy's time of need.

"Annie," Kate said. "Daddy's probably just having bad nightmares. The stuff about the Light—it's not real, Annie. Daddy's just very sick…"

"It *is* real!" Ann exclaimed, balling her hands into stubborn fists. "Don't you see? The Light protected Daddy, and last night it went away! And then that thing came to our house, and today Daddy is sick. Daddy needs his Light back!"

"*…Light…Gap…don't go…she has it…she has it…don't go…don't go…the Light…it's gone…it's gone…*"

Daddy's voice was getting louder as Ann continued to plead her case to Katie, and his breathing was becoming shallower, more labored.

"See? His Light is up at the Gap!" Ann said, rising up from the bed and pointing her finger out the window, toward the mountains that surrounded them at the top of the hollow. Toward the Gap. "Somebody took it. A woman. And we have to go get it back!"

"Annie—"

"No!" Ann stomped her foot and glared at Kate with angry eyes and a runny nose. "I can't believe you don't want to help Daddy get better! He even gave you a special gift last night, before all this happened, and you just want to let him die!"

"YOU SHUT YOUR MOUTH, ANN!" Katie said,

exploding off the bed and stomping over to her petulant child of a sister. "You shut it **RIGHT NOW!**"

"No!" Ann yelled, shoving Kate backwards. "I HATE YOU!"

Kate caught herself on the bed before she could lose her balance and fall to the floor. She made to grab Ann's hair and pull her back, anger surging through her whole body, but her younger sister had already stormed out of the room, past their wide-eyed mother in the door frame, and had slammed her own bedroom door.

Silence fell over the house as Momma put a hand up to her mouth. Even Daddy's whimpering had quieted. Kate said transfixed on Daddy's bed, her heart racing at Ann's hurtful words. Perhaps Kate had been too harsh on her little sister—Ann had only been trying to help.

"...the Light...Gap...she has it...it's gone...she has it...don't go..."

Daddy started up again, drawing Kate out of her thoughts and back into the moment. Her eyes were wet and stinging. She hadn't realized she'd started crying, and she hated the sensation.

Momma sighed loudly from the door, placing her head in her hands and turning back to the hallway, back to her cleaning.

Kate grasped Daddy's hand one more time and squeezed.

"Please get better, Daddy," she said. "Please. Ann needs you. We all need you. *I* need you."

"...the Gap...she has it...she has it...the Light...it's gone...

don't go…don't go…"

Daddy kept his eyes closed as Kate took a moist rag from the night table and wiped the sweat away from his brow, his cheeks, his chin. She replaced the rag and got up to leave, feeling low and defeated at their sudden change in fortune. She couldn't fathom that only last night, they had been a normal family—happy, untainted. And then it had all changed. Now parts of their house lie in ruins, and Daddy looked as though he were at Death's door.

Kate made it to the door and was a step away from leaving the room, but her father gasped behind her. She turned just in time to see him rise straight up out of his reclining position, his eyes wild and horrified as they gazed unflinchingly at her.

Kate backed against the wall, scared at her father's sudden movements, at the horror that washed over his face. Horror that, she could see now, was melting into sadness. Into fatigue. Into unrelenting despair.

"Katie," he whispered, her name barely audible as it passed through his lips. "Remember what I told you."

"Daddy?" Kate said, taking a ginger step back toward his bed.

"Always protect her, Katie," he said. "Always protect your sister. No matter what. You're all each other's got."

A couple minutes later, Momma and Kate were able to calm Daddy back down onto his pillow, where he could rest until the evening doctor returned to check on him one final time before the night.

Kate lie in her bed for the first time since Daddy had woken her the previous night. She fixed her eyes on the window where the hovering orb of light had had been— or where she had *thought* it appeared. Kate was growing more and more skeptical that she had seen anything at all. That part had probably been a dream.

But what came after certainly hadn't been.

There *had* been something in the house. And Daddy had been mortally afraid of it. He had gotten the whole family out of dodge. And Momma's china…and the floors and walls of the house…

There was no denying *something* had happened. Whether it had been an animal, or a burglar, or something easily explain, Kate couldn't say.

What she *did* know was that she had never seen her father this afraid. She had never herself been so afraid for his wellbeing.

She didn't even know how much time had passed since she'd collapsed onto the bed. The thoughts circled through her mind like a horrific merry-go-round—a carousel of terror. She thought about Daddy's stories. About the Light. About how he had told them it followed him home. About how scared he'd been that it was gone.

She thought about Ann. About how badly she wanted to find Daddy's Light in order to save him.

It all sounded so silly.

And *yet*—

Kate couldn't dismiss the Light from her mind. As

her eyelids became heavy weights upon her face, as the light in her room seemed to fade with each passing second, Kate descended into a dreadful sleep. The last thing she remembered seeing before the darkness took her was that same blue, glowing orb hovering outside her window.

• • •

Daddy carried her on his shoulders as he sprinted through the cornfield that sat atop Boomer's Gap. She felt the dead stalks tickle her face as they raced through the familiar place. The cool, crisp air smelled like dying leaves, and the ravens cawed overhead.

"Daddy, faster!" Kate said. Her voice was sweet like honey, the sound of a smile. She was seven years old again. This was the day before Ann was to be born.

"You're going to have a big job starting tomorrow, Katie," Daddy said as they emerged from the dense cornstalks and he slowed into the clearing beyond. "You'll have to look out for your baby sister from here on out, understand?"

"Yes, Daddy," Kate replied innocently, taking his hand as he led them into the dense forest beyond the corn. They climbed and climbed, up the beaten path, Kate's laughter echoing through the woods.

"Ol' Bill, what in the world are you doing up here?" came an unfamiliar voice from behind them.

When Kate turned to see who it belonged to, she saw her father walking toward someone else on the trail. Or—was it *her father?* He was a bit shorter, his frame thinner, and his trademark overalls and flannels had been replaced by a plain white shirt and some brown work pants that hung off of him.

"Arnold Henson, I should've known you'd be scurryin' about up here today," Daddy said, his voice sounding familiar but shallower somehow. He didn't sound like his usual happy self.

When Daddy and the boy named Arnold shook hands, Daddy turned around and Kate could see that he, too, was now a much younger man. He couldn't be more than sixteen. But the features— the baby-blue eyes, the dark hair—were all still there.

"Daddy?" Kate inquired, confused about what she was seeing.

Daddy didn't answer. It was almost as if he couldn't see her at all anymore.

"I was sorry to hear about Sarah," Arnold said. Kate's ears pricked up at the sound of her momma's name. "I thought you might be up here looking for the shack—"

"Keep your voice down," Daddy said. "We're close now. I don't want her to hear me coming."

"Bill, this is dark stuff. Dark magic. It'll cost you something. You know what all the old folks say about her."

"I know well, Arnold. But I love Sarah, and they're saying she won't live to see the dawn. I've got no choice but to try. And this is where she said the Light was."

Arnold stood with his hands in his pockets, chewing on his bottom lip. Kate could tell he seemed awfully uncomfortable.

"Come with me, Arnold," Daddy said. "I need somebody by my side. I'm afraid."

The fear in Daddy's eyes reminded Kate that she was no seven-year-old-girl. She remembered that she was sixteen. She remembered the image of Daddy standing in front of the bathroom mirror, red circles around his eyes, and terrified words coming from his mouth.

The Light. It didn't follow me home tonight.

This is a dream, *Kate told herself.* Just a dream.

Arnold and Daddy hustled off deeper into the forest and, wondering if she might wake up at any moment, she followed them. After a few moments, they picked up their speed.

"Hurry! We don't have much time left!" came her Daddy's strained yells up ahead.

Kate heaved and inhaled sharply and she picked up her pace behind them. Her bare feet sunk into the moist, earthy soil of the mountains as they traversed deeper into the woods.

"Argh!" Kate screamed as a branch snapped back against her face. She could feel a sharp pain just beneath her right eye. She lifted her hand and batted a finger at the skin there, and it came away wet and red.

Blood.

She was sure that would have woken her up. Why wasn't she waking up?

Moments later, she emerged into another clearing. A familiar one. The sight of the cistern, with its black depths, and the worn-down cabin, with its golden light, made her stomach draw in on itself.

No. No. NO!

Daddy and his best friend Arnold stood before the cauldron, before an old hag of a woman dressed in earthen robes that swallowed her whole. Her terrifying face was deeply wrinkled; her mouth was twisted into a wild grin. And one of her eyes bulged from its socket, as though it might pop out at any moment. That one big eye seemed to be transfixed on Kate, while the other eye tracked back and forth from Daddy to Arnold.

Kate took a few steps toward the scene, still hoping her body would force her awake somehow. This was a dream. It had to be.

When Kate was only a few feet away from where the boys stood, they turned in unison to face her, their eyes closed, and their bodies rigid.

The humming started again. The same drone, the same unsettling tones she'd heard in her other dreams. Her eyes scanned the clearing for Ann, since she'd been the one making the sounds the last time, but Kate quickly realized it was the witch's croaking voice that uttered the throaty melody.

Kate watched as Daddy raised one of his arms, palm upward. The witch continued her song and hobbled around the cistern to where Daddy stood.

"Save your love," she said to him in a monotonous murmur that did not seem to interrupt her humming, which continued somewhere in the back of her throat. "Spill innocent blood."

From within her robes, the witch withdrew a long object with a black handle. A dagger, Kate realized.

The hag placed the dagger into Daddy's upturned hand, and his eyes slowly opened. His pupils were wide, far away, entranced.

"Save your love," the witch repeated. "Spill the blood."

"Daddy?" Kate cried, but his expression did not change. His body did not shift or waver. His eyes remained focused straight ahead.

"Save my love," he said, his mouth moving in time with the witch's percussive humming. "Spill the blood."

And without another moments' hesitation, Daddy turned to Arnold and dragged the dagger across his throat, releasing fountains of red that trickled down the young man's neck, onto his white shirt and down to the forest floor.

Kate screamed at the sight of her father taking his best friend's life.

This is a dream. It's just a dream. Wake up, Kate. Wake UP.

The witch let out a guttural laugh and Daddy turned to the cistern, dropping the bloodied blade into its depths. The water inside began to bubble and roil, and the inky darkness began to illuminate, a familiar blue glow rising from its depths.

The witch, still laughing, pointed pale, bony fingers at Arnold's body—somehow he had managed to remain standing—as his own hands grasped at the open wound at his throat. Ruby-red tendrils streaked down the backs of his palms and flowed down to his arms. His eyes were open now, too, and they were fixed on Daddy.

Fear and betrayal colored Arnold's gaze as Daddy turned back to face him.

Arnold didn't make a sound as his feet hovered off the ground. The witch's laughter echoed through the treetops as she waved her arms to and fro, some unseen magic driving her prey airborne.

Kate's knees collapsed, her body still unwilling to wake her from this nightmare, and she watched from the ground as Arnold's body was floated just above the cauldron.

The witch began to utter words that Kate could not understand, soft at first, but each phrase growing in malice and volume. Daddy backed away from the scene, placing a hand over his mouth. Kate caught a quick glimpse of his pale eyes—now horrified at what had taken place. He had lured his friend to this place only to kill him. And for what?

But Kate already knew why he'd done it. Somehow it had all come together in her head.

"This guitar pick was given to me by my best buddy Arnold, many years ago," *Daddy had said.* "He was like a brother to me, and in some ways I think he's still taking care of me to this day."

As Kate turned it all over in her mind, the witch's chants seemed to compound, causing her voice to rumble the very earth upon which they all stood. The trees seemed to bend toward her, crackling and snapping within the deep forest that surrounded the clearing.

No, that wasn't the trees that were crackling and snapping. It was Arnold. It was his bones.

Arnold let out a gurgling sound as his body turned upside down over the cistern, the blood from his neck dripping into the glowing water below. For a moment, the bright-blue glow phased into a deep red, and then back again.

The witch shouted her final words and clenched her hands into tight fists. When Kate looked back to Arnold's hovering body, she watched and listened as his spine snapped and his body folded in on itself. Both Daddy and Kate let out a terrified yell, tears streaming from their eyes, and Arnold's maimed and broken body plopped into the large cauldron with a splash.

The clearing went quiet. The light from the cauldron faded. The witch turned her head to Daddy, her bulging eye scanning his terrified face.

"I have fulfilled the bargain, William," she said. "You will find Sarah in perfect health when you return to her."

With that, the witch turned and hobbled back toward her rickety shack, silhouetted against the golden light permeating from the open door.

Daddy sat breathless on the ground, his head in his hands, unable to contain the tears, the emotions, at what he'd just done.

"I'm so sorry, I'm so sorry," he said over and over. "Arnold…"

A sizzling sound, like Momma's pressure cooker when it was going full steam, caused Kate and Daddy to turn back to the cauldron in time to see a glowing orb rising from within. The orb shined bright-blue in the darkened clearing, with ethereal tendrils that seemed to guide its motion in the air.

The orb floated over to Daddy, illuminating his glassy eyes. He breathed in deeply, aghast at the sight. As the orb drew closer to him, Daddy peered into the light, a hint of familiarity crossing his face.

"Arnold?" he said. "Arnold is that you?"

Kate watched as Daddy peered into the blue light, but with each passing moment, the image faded and moved farther and farther away from her.

"Daddy?" she called, scared to be leaving his side. She reached out his hand to try and grasp him, but Daddy and the Light were mere dots in a sea of blackness.

• • •

W hen Kate woke, she found herself drenched in sweat and curled up on a patch of mossy forest floor, a bright moon shining overhead.

"Daddy?" she called, wondering if she might have woken up back in her dreams again. The last thing she remembered before falling asleep was being in her own bed, reflecting on all the horrors that had befallen her family in the last day.

"Where——"

Kate didn't have time to get the other words out before she felt her body being violently dragged across the wet, dead leaves that lined the forest floor.

"Stop!" she cried, stinging pain flaring up all over her body. "Help me! Help!"

Whatever had hold of her was fast, insatiable. She heard it growl above her——guttural, feral. Kate had no way to know where she was, as the forest clipped past in a blur. She could only glimpse the creature that carried her off, as it passed through intermittent beams of moonlight that shone through the treetops.

It was gargantuan, several heads taller than an average man, and it seemed to be dragging her with one arm, while it started through the brush on two long, bony legs.

When it finally came to a halt, it turned its face toward her and hovered just over her body. Kate's breath caught in her chest and her stomach roiled at the sight of the creature's lidless black eyes. Its pupils were small and sickly-white; they looked like marbles floating in a sea of tar. Its nose was flat, triangular, with two slitted nostrils that expanded and contracted as it breathed. And its mouth was wide——a gaping maw concealing a row of sharp, razor-like teeth.

"What are you?" Kate cried, her voice weak and piti-ful, drowning in an ocean of her fear.

The creature threw back its head and let out a roar—the same roar the family had heard from their basement when the creature had left the house last night.

Kate hid her face in her hands, cowering in fear as the sound sliced into the otherwise quiet night.

When the cacophony subsided, she heard the creature shift as it moved away from her. She kept her eyes tightly shut, dreading the thought of seeing the monster again. When she was finally brave enough to open them, she realized where the creature had brought her.

"We've been expecting you, Kate," came a familiar croaking voice.

Kate sat up straight, an acrid smell filling her nose—like pine sap and rotten fruit.

"The last Light fades, and a new Light must take its place," came the witch's voice.

Kate turned to see the cistern, right where she expect-ed it would be, in front of the witch's ramshackle dwell-ing. She was high atop Boomer's Gap, where Kate's dreams had taken her of late.

The witch stood before the vast cauldron, her arms spread wide, one bulging eye staring straight at Kate.

"How do you know my name?" Kate said. "I've never met you before."

"Oh, but you have," the witch said, taking a few steps forward toward Kate. Kate hustled to her feet, trying to keep distance between herself and the haggard-looking woman, but the witch balled her right hand into a fist, and Kate's feet felt as though they'd been set stubbornly into a cement block.

She was helpless.

"I've met you many times in your dreams, Kate," the witch cooed softly, but with an understated ferocity. "Sometimes you were aware, and sometimes you weren't. But all has led you here to me tonight."

The witch raised both of her arms and Kate felt her body lifting off the ground, suddenly weightless in the chilly mountain air. The witch floated her toward the cistern and placed her gently down on the soil, which was cold against Kate's bare feet. A gentle breeze rustled in the trees, and Kate suddenly felt a chill shift beneath the thin cotton of her pajamas.

"What do you want from me?" Kate asked nervously, all resolve falling away from her voice.

"I don't want anything, young one," the witch replied. "Someone else has made a request of me, as they always do. And you're here to help me fulfill that request."

At that moment, the pale, gangly creature that had dragged Kate to the clearing materialized from the tree line at the far end. Kate could see it better now—its disproportionate limbs, its large, walnut-shaped head, seated between spiny shoulders. It looked gaunt, like a wounded animal. Sharp, talon-like claws extended from long, slender fingers and toes.

"What is that thing?" Kate asked, her heart pounding in her ears. She didn't want the creature to come any closer to her than it already was.

"Oh, that poor soul? My dear, that is why you're here. For many years now, this creature has served a very specific purpose. And now his time as the Light has come to an end."

Kate tried to digest her words, tried to make them make sense, but she couldn't make heads or tails of what she had heard. Her face must have given her away, because the ugly hag moved to stand in front of her and, with a devious smile, opened her mouth to continue.

"You see, your father made a bargain with me a long time ago," she said. "You saw it, I believe. I showed you. In your dreams. And for almost three decades, that bargain has held."

The pale creature let out a short cry, and Kate noticed its breath was visible in the cold. It hung its head pitifully as the witch spoke, as if in pain.

"But, as I explained to your father all those year ago—on a night much like this one—no bargain is forever," the witch said, turning away from Kate and walking around to the other side of the cistern.

Kate's feet still felt heavy; she didn't think she'd get very far if she ran. But she was able to turn and keep her eyes on the crone.

"Your father, as I hear it, is now quite ill," the witch said.

"Yes," Kate replied. "The doctors don't know what's wrong with him. He's dying."

The witch drew her lips into a taut grin, accentuating

the wrinkles around her nose and mouth.

"Come on out, dear," she said, leaving Kate to wonder if she'd been referring to Kate herself.

A moment later, Kate heard a latch click behind the witch. The door to her rickety shack began to swing open, bathing a crescent of the clearing in the orange light that glowed from within.

"No," Kate whispered when she saw the shadowy silhouette of a young girl standing in the doorway. "Ann, get away from here! Go home now and find Momma!"

The familiar shape of her little sister walked into the light of the clearing, her face no longer obscured. Her eyes were sad, as if she'd been crying, and her auburn hair disheveled.

As Ann made her way to the cistern, Kate tried to back away from it, fighting against the invisible weights holding her feet in place. The sad creature—the one that was somehow tied to this whole mess—wailed from the other side of the clearing, letting out a howl that disturbed the quiet of the surrounding woods.

"I did it for Daddy," Ann said, her voice timid, but her eyes suddenly locking onto Kate, sending a wave of guilt through her gut.

"Ann, we need to get away from here," Kate said, pleading. "We need to go home and take care of Daddy. I'm sorry for upsetting you, and we can talk about it, but first we need to run."

"You'll not be going anywhere, my dear," croaked the witch as she reached into her cloak and pulled out an object Kate had seen quite recently.

It was the dagger from her dream. The one she'd watched her father use to slice open his friend Arnold's throat.

The lake creature let out another howl. Kate looked over as it's clawed hands reached up to its neck, rubbing and caressing at some invisible wound, as if the sight of the blade brought back terrible memories—terrible pain.

Arnold, Kate suddenly understood. *The creature is Arnold.*

"And now, we begin," the witch states plainly, closing the gap between herself and Ann.

"No! Ann, no!" Kate screamed as the witch placed the blade into Ann's upturned palm. The younger girl looked down at the dagger as if she couldn't fathom what she might do with such an instrument of death.

"Ann!" Kate screamed again. The witch cocked her neck to peer at Kate, the crone's devious grin morphing into one of pure evil, as if Kate's pleas and desperate cries were hopeless.

"Ann, Daddy didn't want this!" Kate screamed. Ann looked up from the dagger. The witch shifted her focus to Ann, suddenly concerned.

It had hit Kate like a ton of bricks. In all the nonsense Daddy had been talking, he had been trying to communicate a message to the girls. He had mentioned the Light. He had mentioned the Gap. He had even implicated the witch—*she has it.*

But he had also been adamant in telling them to stay away: *Don't go,* he'd said. *Don't go.* Over and over and over,

Daddy had told them not to go.

"This is what he meant, Ann!" Kate shouted to her sister, forcing her feet to carry her around the giant tub so that she could stand beside her sister. So that she could try and pry the knife out of her hands.

"He meant for us to stay away from this place. He told us not to go! He meant for it to end with him!"

Ann looked up at Kate, fear suddenly filling her wide eyes. Kate watched the moisture pool, as tears glistened, ready to fall at any moment.

"I had a vision, Ann," Kate said, casting a quick glance back over to the creature—to Arnold. "It's all real. The Light, Daddy's guardian angel—it's all real! I'm sorry I didn't believe you!"

"Silence!" the witch cawed, hobbling over to where they stood, her arms raised. Kate felt herself go rigid again, unable to move or even speak. The crone turned her bulging gaze to Ann. "You know what to do, my dear."

Ann's glassy eyes tracked down to the blade in her hand, and then back up to Kate. From behind them, Kate could hear the pitiful, misshapen creature howling into the night, unsettling the forest.

"Do it now!" bellowed the witch. "Spill the blood! Save your love!"

Everything happened quickly then. Kate barely registered Ann's movement as the younger girl twisted away from the witch and climbed the outer wall of the cistern, submerging her body in the dark water within.

"Child!" the witch called. "What is the meaning of this treachery?"

Kate's eyes shifted from the old hag back to Ann, who lifted the dagger with a shaky hand, her sad eyes examining it, turning it over, studying its sharp edges.

"Katie," Ann called from within the cauldron. "I'm sorry. I stole it from you."

Kate stood perplexed, unsure of what she should do, whether or not she should intervene and try to get Ann out of the cistern so that they could run away. Ann simply reached into the front pocket of her thin pajama top and pulled out a small, triangular object.

"I was jealous Daddy gave it to you and not me," Ann said, tossing the guitar pick to the ground in front of Kate's feet. "I'm sorry for everything."

Kate bent down to retrieve the pick, feeling the sting of tears clawing away at her eyes, forcing themselves over, and crawling down her cold cheeks.

"Ann, I—"

The witch let out a guttural yell, and hobbled toward the cistern. Kate made to stop her, but a pale blur zoomed by her and tackled the old hag to the dirty ground. Her screams mixed with the creature's feral growls as it lashed at her sides and face with its claws, clamping its jowls down on her aging form, the disgusting sounds of cracking bones reaching Kate's ears.

Kate looked back to Ann, just in time to see fresh tears cascading from her big, innocent eyes. But there was a knowing in those eyes now. A banishment. The little girl who had resided in Ann's body was no more. Kate could see that it was a much more mature, responsible person making the decisions now.

"Save my love," Ann said.

"No!" Kate shouted, leaping across the distance that separated her from the cistern.

But it was too late.

"Spill the blood..."

Before Kate's feet could touch the ground, Ann had plunged the dagger into her own chest, her face tightening in horror, in unadulterated pain.

"Ann, oh God! No!" Kate's screams tore into the darkness above and around them as the water in the cauldron began to roil and rage.

"Ann!" Kate reached over the walls of the cistern and grabbed her little sister by the hands, but Ann couldn't hold on. Kate moved her hands to the gaping wound in Ann's chest, trying to stifle the crimson flow that escaped into the water below. Ann kept her gaze tight on Kate as the water spun about her like a cyclone. The wind blew through the trees and a roaring rumble reverberated above them.

A miserable yelping sound stunned Kate, forcing her to turn her head to the right, where she saw the pale creature shifting in pain. His features were morphing before her eyes as he writhed along the ground. Disproportionate limbs turned into human arms and legs. Fearsome black eyes turned into human brown ones. The flat, slotted nose turned into one that looked much like her own, though perhaps broken a few times.

Arnold, Daddy's best friend. His teenage self preserved and lying on the forest floor next to the witch's unmoving body.

"Katie, take care of Daddy," Ann said, and Kate looked back to her, shaking her and begging her.

"No! Ann, no! You have to get out of there, we can fix it! We can get the doctor—"

But the water had risen, tiny tendrils from within had already latched themselves onto Ann's body. They were overtaking her, pulling her under.

"You have to let go, Katie," Ann said, her voice faint in the loud roar permeating the night. "Let go."

At last, Kate had no choice. The force of the water, of the tendrils that surrounded her sister, pushed Katie away from the cistern, and Ann's body was yanked beneath the surface, and down into the inky depths.

"No! Ann! NO! NO!"

Kate's screams tore through her as she fell backward onto the dirty soil in front of the cistern, and quickly turned to sobs.

As soon as she craned her head upward again, she saw, through her tears, a brilliant blue glow emanating from the cauldron. She heard the water bubble and roil as it sloshed against the cistern's wooden sides. A moment later, a luminous orb arose from the tub, tiny blue tendrils of ethereal fog surrounding it and guiding its hovering path.

Kate heard a crackling noise near her, and when she

looked over, Arnold's body had been illuminated in the same blue glow. Tiny veins traced themselves all over his skin, and the light illuminated the patterns as they spread. Seconds later, the crackling noise grew louder, and in a flash, Arnold's body disintegrated, extinguishing the blue light as turned to dirt and sand.

The orb hovered a moment over the cistern and then fluttered over to Kate. It drew near her face, as if studying her, really looking at her.

As if it knew her.

Kate remembered her dream, remembered how Daddy had recognized Arnold after he'd become the Light.

The last Light fades, the witch had said. *And a new Light must take its place.*

Kate let out shallow breaths she hadn't realized she'd been holding, sudden understanding washing over her.

Ann was the new Light. She'd taken Arnold's place. And she had sacrificed herself to do so.

"Ann," Kate whispered into the glow, and then she felt fresh, hot tears falling down both cheeks. "Oh, Ann, I'm so sorry."

Kate let her head fall between her knees and grasped her brown locks, at a loss. She let her sobs out unabashedly, thinking of all that had transpired.

When she looked up again, Ann was still there, hovering. The Light moved over the spot of grass where the witch had been felled, but the old hag's body was gone. In fact, so was her shack. So was the cistern.

All of it.

Vanished without a trace.

Kate sat transfixed, looking around the clearing for some kind of answer. Some kind of instructions. But there was only brush and dirt and the sound of crickets chirping in the distance, ravens cawing in the trees.

The Light flew back to her, hovering mere inches from her face. Kate let herself look into its blue depths, hoping she might see the face of her sister. Hear her voice.

She saw nothing. She heard nothing.

But what she *felt*, she could not explain.

It was a warmth. A calm peace. She felt a sense of continuation. Like she could move from this spot, make her way back home. Like she had the strength to face whatever came next.

She didn't know how she'd explain what had happened. She didn't know how she'd tell Momma and Daddy that Ann wasn't coming home with her.

At least, not in the way they expected her to.

The Light hovered away from Kate and over to the path that led back home, as if beckoning Kate to follow. As if saying *I'm your guardian angel. I'll protect you now.*

Kate rose, drying her tears with the backs of her hands and taking one last look around the clearing. She couldn't discern what had happened to the witch. She hoped this would be the last night she'd ever see her, but she imagined the old crone would haunt her dreams for years to come.

Kate turned from the clearing, never more eager to

be out of the dark woods. She stepped onto the trail where the Light waited for her—where *Ann* waited—and together, they began the long walk home.

DUSTIN STREET is an author, publisher, educator, and dog dad who grew up surrounded by stories in the Appalachian mountain town of Erwin, Tennessee. He writes with a passion for sharing those stories, and more. He recently opened a new publishing company, Big Small Town Books, in hopes of amplifying the voices of storytellers in Appalachia and beyond. He has two stories published in anthologies released by the Unicoi County High School Creative Writing Club, where he mentors young writers and helps them navigate first-time publication.

HAVEN

DENVER MUNCEY

HENRY

I slowly rubbed my fingers over the oak wood of my weathered bedroom door. The room smelled of old pine and stayed uncomfortably hot. I lay on my bed, the covers stripped and in the floor.

Silence.

At least that was the usual. No noise. Sometimes there was the occasional mocking chirp of the birds that nested in the gutters of our log cabin. My father and I lived alone for - well, I had stopped counting. I hated it. But, he had it built for us, so I would always put on a fake smile for him. As I lay down in the stiffest bed I had ever laid in, I looked at the wall. The yellow light of my flickering lamp illuminated the etchings I had made in it to signify a day's passing.

I stopped counting at 925. 925 days since he started locking me up in my room and giving me all these extra rules. Counting won't get us out of here.

My father knew I counted, but it's the one thing he let me do without questioning. No matter what, I needed a reason for even the smallest of actions. Going out for a hike in the woods, exploring the rocks down by the river, or even writing in a journal. Going into the basement was completely off-limits. I didn't ask why; I was too scared of what he might think if I did. He was merely the textbook overprotective father.

But like every father, he had his ticks.

The lock clicked on my bedroom door, and it creaked open. "You'll need to turn on the music tonight, Henry," Dad said gruffly. Music at night—one of his ticks.

My father had a stern way about him. Ever since Mom left, he would just sit alone in his recliner mindlessly clicking through the channels. If the weather was nice, sometimes he would hunt. He's never brought anything back for us.

"Yessir," I muttered quietly.

He gave me a long look, almost sadness. He shut the door, locking it from the outside. I slunk from my bed and walked over to the small radio sitting on my cabinet. I filed through the box of discs my father had bought me for occasions like this. I wasn't allowed to play it unless he demanded. I didn't really know why he always wanted me to play music. Maybe it was to block out a noise from his ears? Maybe it was to block a noise from mine? I was too scared to ask.

I pulled '80's Greatest Hits from the stack and put it in. I cranked the volume to full blast as he expected.

I hobbled back to my bed, climbed in, and closed my eyes. The music pierced my ears, sending shocks of pain through my head with every beat of a drum. I pulled a pillow over my head and pressed hard against me ears, trying to drown out whatever noise I could.

This was life, and I had to accept that.

This was home.

I dreaded sleep when the music was on; it always gave me the worst nightmare. But I knew soon my father would check on me and make sure I was asleep, so I had no choice.

• • •

H enry...Henry...WAKE UP!"

A deformed voice echoed loudly, and my eyes shot open.

I was lying on the forest floor breathing heavily. I looked around from my position on the damp mossy ground.

Darkness.

Get up, it's that dream again, I thought to myself.

I slowly stood up, my bones aching from being still for so long. Never had the dream given me pain like that. It was real, too real. I saw the faint light of the cabin in the distance. The dream always began and ended in the same place.

I would wake up on the ground, stand up, and walk back into my bed. When I first had the dream, I'd try and fight my path. But, eventually, I learned that I couldn't. It was the same every time.

I took my time, watching the scenery around me as my eyes adjusted. This dream was really the only time I ever saw the outside world during the night. Like every other night in this dream, I could hear the whispers. The whispers are what always scared me. That's what I wanted to fight, wanted to run from, but I couldn't. They followed me closely, but not close enough to where I could always understand them. They were just tiny whispers from behind trees and in bushes.

"He's the boy. The son," I would hear from time to time.

My mind had become a master at playing tricks on me. The dreams, the whispers, the mind-games—it was something I got used to.

It wasn't long before I had made it to the cabin. The dream was ending.

I shuffled slowly to the front porch of the cabin, swung around the corner, and my father stood there, watching me.

"Dad?" He had not been in this dream before.

"Why are you outside, Son?" He asked me sternly, gripping a shotgun in his left hand.

"I—I ju—just—"

"Get inside, Boy," He said as he ushered me through the front door.

We walked inside silently, my father behind me. I heard the front door slam shut. I sat on the couch, keeping as still as I possibly could. He sat in front of me, giving me a long stare. I dusted off some leaves that were on my pajamas.

"Why are you dirty?" My father snapped at me.

"I woke up outside," I replied, not really thinking before I spoke.

He was taken aback, completely thrown off from what I had said. He knelt down to me after a moment. "You don't just wake up outside, Henry."

"Yessir." The only words I could spit out, almost by instinct.

"Yessir? I am not correcting you. I am telling you what does not happen. Little boys just don't disappear from their bedrooms and end up in the woods." He leaned in towards me, "I wanna know what the hell you were doing in that forest."

I froze, my body beginning to shake. I couldn't speak back to him. He threw his massive hand on my shoulder, squeezed tight, and pulled me closer.

"I am looking for an answer, Son," he whispered

aggressively in my ear.

"I don't know. . ." My voice quivered.

My father stood up, grabbed the shotgun, and walked over to the door. He gestured to it, pointing the gun towards the doorknob. "There is nothing for you out there. There is nothing for us out there. Don't let your mother's spirit sway you like that again. You're a lot like her. . . She always had a knack for adventurous things."

He only ever brought up my mother when I was being like her, or if I was in trouble. This time, it was both.

"Go to your room. Turn off the music if you're having trouble sleeping." He motioned to my bedroom door.

I let out a sigh of relief.

"Thanks, Dad," I said as I walked towards my room. I peeked at him quietly before shutting the door.

"Goodnight, Henry," he replied.

"Goodnight." I slowly crawled back into my bed.

The door locked, and I tried as hard as I could to go back to sleep.

• • •

DAVID

I crawled into my bed slowly, my arms and legs aching from the day's work. Keeping the cabin in order was my only true responsibility, next to keeping my son safe.

A good night's rest was always necessary just to complete those jobs every day. My head hit the pillow softly. As it hit the comfortable cotton and fabric, a deafening ring filled the room. I knew the sound well.

The phone.

I sprinted out of my bed, nearly falling to the ground as I tangled myself in the sheets. I grabbed the phone as I stumbled to my knees.

"Emergencies only, Reverend." I whispered, trying not to wake up my son.

"It's been a while, David. I'm just making sure all is well up on the mountain." The local pastor answered in his stern but comforting voice.

The statement infuriated me. I had done everything in my power to keep the phone a secret from Henry, and Reverend Thomas knew that.

"Yeah, I'm fine. Everything is fine," I assured him.

"Good, good," he responded. I could tell something was on his mind.

"So. . ." I waited.

"Can you come down tonight, David? It's just that we haven't spoken in a while, and I get worried. . ."

I hated leaving if it wasn't absolutely necessary, but the last thing I needed was Reverend Thomas coming after me. I caved.

"Alright, I'll be there. Just, please, don't call here unless you have to," I said angrily.

I pulled on a ragged pair of blue jeans, pulled on my coat, grabbed my cap, and walked out of my bedroom. The cabin smelled of pine and mildew. It had been a while since it's last deep clean. I walked over to Henry's door.

Knock. Knock. Knock.

"I'm heading to the store. Be back soon."

Silence. Of course.

I shook my head and walked out the front door and hopped into my old pickup truck. The thing made a god-awful noise every time I would try and start it up. Any animal within a mile radius would've been spooked by it. Finally, the engine started, grumbling, waiting to be gassed up.

I took off into the foggy winter night, straight towards the old chapel.

My truck was a race horse, driving a full on eighty-five miles per hour consistently without any issues. She was always trusty and had been for thirty-two years now. The dense mist created a dark gray wall that seemed inescapable. It felt supernatural in the way that it never faltered.

I slung my truck into the chapel's parking lot, kicking

up gravel into the yard. It was quite possibly my favorite thing to do in the old truck.

I stepped out, a huge grin on my face. I always felt like I needed to put a face on for Reverend Thomas. He'd ask too many questions if I didn't. Gravel dust filled the air, and I could hear coughs from around the other side of my truck. Out of the darkness, Reverend Thomas emerged. He waved the smoky debris out of his face and eyes.

"Mr. Larr," he said through light coughs, "I think it's time that we talk."

• •

I followed Reverend Thomas through the massive chapel doors. As they slowly opened, an ear-piercing screech echoed through the church. The church was old, built in the early 1900's. It smelled of old pine and candle wax. Reverend Thomas sat in the pew at the very front of the church.

"It's been too long." Reverend Thomas's booming voice filled the church.

"It has." I responded, and he was right.

Years ago, I would've always gone to Reverend Thomas when something was on my mind. Things happened, I got busy, and now I don't. It's nobody's fault. I could tell he was trying to start a conversation, but I wasn't much of a chatty person.

"I just thought we should catch up," he said.

"At eleven o'clock at night?" I asked.

He looked down at his Bible, clutching it tightly.

"Sometimes you just get a feeling, David. Something is on your mind, isn't it?" He looked at me with an expression in his eyes I had not seen before.

"I—I don't know what you want me to say, Reverend—" I fumbled over my words.

I wiped a nervous sweat suddenly swelling on my brow. I didn't know what Reverend Thomas knew, and I sure as hell wasn't going to open up to him.

"Yes, David. You do." He grabbed my knee tightly.

• • •

HENRY

I heard Dad's truck roar off into the night moments after I tried going back to bed.

The dream was *real* this time. I had never experienced anything like it. The dreams were always vivid, but never had they actually been real.

Knock. Knock. Knock.

"Yeah?" I asked, assuming my father was on the other

side. I thought I had heard him leave, but maybe I was dreaming then? The vividness of my dreams had never created this much confusion in my head.

Knock. Knock. Knock.

I stood up, but didn't approach the door.

"Dad?" I yelled a little louder.

Knock. Knock. Knock.

I padded up to the door slowly. I put my hand on the doorknob and twisted, fully expecting it not to budge, locked.

The door unlatched and swung open.

My heart pounded. This door was *never* open without Dad being there to open it.

"Hey, Dad," I called out into the silence of the cabin. Nothing.

I walked out into the living room and heard a crack under my foot as I took my first step across the threshold, and a slight pinch shot through it. As I lifted my foot, a pawn from my chessboard was snapped perfectly in half. As I looked around, I saw the remainder of my chess pieces delicately arranged in a line connecting my bedroom door to the front door, ending with a standing King and the Queen knocked over on her side. The sight shocked me. Had I been sleepwalking again? I immediately began retracing my steps to try and remember if I was the one who had done this. It couldn't have been me.

I slowly walked to the front door, picking up my chess pieces one by one. I frequently would play chess against myself just for the fun of it. I wasn't able to do anything outside on my own, so I was forced to come up with creative pastimes.

I put all my collected pieces on a small table by the door. I slowly opened the rickety screen door and felt the cool breeze of a winter's night roll over my face like a tidal wave. The outside at night. The place that I had been so strictly forbidden from was right in front of me now. The trees waved with the breeze and an owl sang into the night.

I slipped on a jacket and some shoes and took a confident step onto the porch. It felt wrong to do, but I never got the opportunity to explore on my own. My dad had not only forbid me from exploring the woods, but he never told me about them either. He hated talking about them for some reason. Any time I asked him, he'd fall silent. Now, if I explored them, I'd never have to ask him again; I'd find out on my own.

The snow fell hard upon the forest floor. It was the first time I had ever seen it from the outside since my father started locking me in my room. I only ever got to watch the snow through my window. I had forgotten what if felt like. It hit my hand lightly and covered my clothes in a soft layer of white. The snow dampened my hands as I held them out to catch the flakes, the icy coolness numbing my hands slowly. Dad said we were gonna get up to seven inches overnight. I took slow steps as I stumbled over the patches of snow.

That's when I heard them. The whispers. I could barely make out what they were saying.

"Him." They would say.

"Watch." I heard another.

I stopped in my tracks and looked around me. The towering silhouettes of the large pines loomed over me in the skies, like massive giants staring down at me. My heart pounded from excitement and dread as I made my way deeper into the forest. The moonlight faintly lit the area around me. I looked around for any sign of the whispers. Nobody to be seen.

"Hey?" I yelled into the pitch black.

I waited silently.

"Keep walking, Henry."

• • •

DAVID

I honestly have no idea what the hell you're talking about." I stood up quickly, pushing his hand off my knee.

Reverend Thomas walked towards the back of the church, and into his office. I reluctantly followed. He rummaged around his desk drawer, pulled out a polaroid, and handed it to me.

"Mandy." I muttered under my breath.

Mandy Larr was the most amazing woman a person could ever meet. We got married. Built the cabin together. Raised Henry for what little time she was here. It wasn't fair that she—

"That was taken the first time you ever visited the church," said Reverend Thomas.

I smiled. That was a rarity these days.

"Look, David," Reverend Thomas approached me. "It's been two years now—"

"I know how long it's been." I glared at him, finally breaking my gaze from the picture.

"All I'm saying is that you never really got the chance to talk about it. You spend all that time up there on the mountain with Henry. I just think it's time that you let it out."

I shoved the picture in my pocket. "You don't want that," I said as I left his office and stormed into the chapel area.

"No. I do. It's important." He followed after me.

I slung open the church door, the screech piercing my ears and the snow immediately blanketing my face. I turned to him.

"She's gone." I yelled over the whipping winds. "I've accepted that."

"I don't think you have," he said to me.

I shook my head, pulled my hat over my forehead to block the snow from my eyes, and walked to my truck.

"David, please."

I got in the driver's seat and fired it up. The truck let out a squeal that would've woken anyone up from their sleep. I rolled down the window. Reverend Thomas stood in the snow, the lights behind him flickering on and off.

"Thank you for the picture. I need to get home." Then, I pulled off onto the narrow street, slamming the gas pedal.

• • •

HENRY

I spun around to find the voice that had just said my name.

No way anyone is up here, I thought.

I began my trek back to the cabin. If Dad caught me, I'd never leave that room.

"Turn around," a voice whispered.

"You aren't done," said another, louder and as if it were right behind me.

The whispers became like a swarm, as if an army surrounded me. I kept my eyes facing forward; I wasn't turning around for anything. I could see the cabin not too far away—the front door open and the lights inside pulling me back home.

"Come back." The voices were getting much louder

now.

I bolted for the door; I wasn't getting caught by whatever monsters were waiting in the woods. I took two steps onto the porch, put my hand out to open the screen door, and then it hit me.

I ran into something hard, like a hand slamming into my chest, and I fell to the porch, the breath completely knocked out of my lungs. I gasped for air and peered up into the doorway. A towering shadow stood over me, eyes as white as the snow laying on the ground. His muscular build took up the entirety of the doorway. He stared at me intensely for a long moment before: "Go back." A deformed voice came from the shadow.

The boom of the voice jolted me from my disorientation; I got to my feet quickly and began my sprint away from the cabin. I didn't care where I ended up, as long as I was away from the Shadow Man. I could barely see ahead of me, but as I looked around, I could see bright white pairs of eyes surrounding me, practically glowing in the forest.

"Run, Henry. Get away," they said in unison.

I quickly approached a large pine that blocked my path. I grasped onto it. As I looked up the large wooden tower, I closed my eyes, and began to ascend the enormous tree, hoping desperately that whatever the voices came from couldn't climb trees.

...

DAVID

S moke blew from my muffler as I sped down the winding Appalachian roads. I pulled the picture from my pocket and held it tightly in my hand as I drove. Reverend Thomas was a good man, and he meant well, but there were some things a person didn't need to know.

I glanced down at the picture, down at Mandy. As I did, I heard a deafening *bang*, and the wheel ripped itself from my hands. I slammed harshly into the guardrail. Glass from my smashed windshield suddenly littered the seats and my lap. I grabbed my throbbing head and felt the wetness of fresh blood on my fingertips.

"Dammit," I muttered angrily.

I opened the door and slowly eased myself out of the car. I sat on the pavement, smoke now billowing from the hood of the truck and the headlights flickering. I nestled my head in my hands.

That's when I heard them. The wailing sirens approaching from the road ahead of me. Coming for me. I attempted to pull myself from the ground, using my truck to no avail.

The police car angled itself in front of me, and a man exited the vehicle. A young man, mid-twenties, with thick brown hair.

"Deputy Britton," he introduced as he approached me. "Got the call and got here as soon as I could."

They didn't send backup? I wondered to myself as I grabbed the arm he extended to help me to my feet. *And what call?* The only person I could possibly think of was Reverend Thomas.

"Thank you," I said. "Lost control of the wheel, hit my head pretty hard."

"Yessir. Let's get you into the car," he said as he grabbed hold of me so I could use him as support.

"That won't be necessary." I said, "I just need a ride back to my house."

He chuckled. "Sir, you need to get to a hospital as soon as possible."

I pushed him off of me. There was no choice to be made. I *had* to get back to my son.

"No, I don't need a hospital." I told him, "No, unless you can fix my truck, or give me a ride, I won't be needing your assistance tonight."

He gave me a concerned look. Slowly, he walked over to my truck, popped open the hood, and peered inside.

There it was. His pistol, glimmering in its holster, beckoning me. I was containing every urge that I had to just lunge forward and grab it. To hold it. To feel the cold metal. I shook my head harshly, attempting to get those old thoughts out of my head.

"This engine is fried," Deputy Britton said, his voice muffled from talking into the hood.

"Figured as much," I said as I approached him.

I just need his keys. That's all I need. Just to get in his car and get home. To see my son. To make sure he's safe.

I saw the outline of the keys in his pocket. I took a few steps closer, extended my arm, and grabbed for the keys. He jerked around, and stared at me in shock. He put his hands up.

"Whoa, hey." He said nervously, his eyes locked on my hand.

I looked down to see the gun grasped in my hand. I couldn't drop it. It was like it *had* to be there. I was in as much shock as he was. I could feel my grip involuntarily tightening

BLAM!

The pistol fell gracefully out of my hand and bounced on the ground. I looked up slowly, only to see Deputy Britton grasping his chest. Blood crept from behind his hand, darkening his tan shirt as it spread like wildfire. He glanced down in disbelief as he pulled his hand away from his chest and out towards me, seeing his own blood on his trembling hand. I watched the life drain from eyes as he fell against my truck and ever so slowly slipped to the ground. I calmly analyzed the all-too-familiar expression of a soul moving on.

He hit the ground, his breath shortening. I walked over to him, searched his pockets for the keys, grabbed them, and approached his police car.

I looked back. Britton laid on the ground, his eyes finally glossed over.

I piled into the cop car, the keys fumbling out of my hand as I attempted to put them into the ignition. It had been so long since something like that happened to me.

I finally started the car, and drove off into the night.

• • •

HENRY

As I climbed, I peered down at the forest floor below. I grabbed a large limb above me and pulled.

SNAP!

The limb ripped from the tree, throwing my balance as it plummeted. I fell for what felt like an eternity.

I landed in a hard heap on the frozen forest floor, a sharp pain suddenly piercing and burning in my abdomen. The branch was buried deep into my side. Blood gushed onto my pajamas and stained the white snow red.

I shoved my fist in my mouth and bit down, choking back a scream; I couldn't scream for help. What if Dad heard me? What if *they* heard me?

The cabin was only a few yards away. I began my slow crawl. Every movement of my arm sent shockwaves of sharp pains down my ribcage, the deformed branch digging into the skin. I could feel the warm crimson running down my side, the smell of pennies filling my nostrils.

My eyes began to get heavy. I was losing it; the dark night crept into my vision and tried to force me under.

Keeping moving. Just keep moving.

I couldn't. I reached my arm out towards a small tree, using every ounce of strength to pull myself closer to the cabin.

The cabin, the place I spent my whole life trying to leave, was now my safe haven. So close, but not close enough.

I pulled hard with my left arm to inch closer, and I let out a yelp of pain.

Then I heard the running.

Dad? I began to power my way forward, yelling out in pain with every move of my muscles. He would find me, but it was a matter of getting to the cabin first.

The footsteps became faster, louder.

Go. Go. Go.

I clutched the water hose stretching out from the house and used it to pull myself closer. Now I just had to get to the porch. I clung to the outside wall and began to pull myself to my feet. With what little strength I had left, I forced myself to lean on the side of the house. With every step, daggers of burning pain shot from my side, through my waist, and down my leg. My eyes drooped even heavier now. The footsteps were getting quicker. He was right behind me.

I had to face him now. With courage, I swung myself around.

Nothing. Just the woods.

"Keep going, Henry," I heard a soft voice say.

I collapsed to the ground in fear, the sharp pains momentarily disorienting my vision. When it cleared, that's when I saw her.

Standing tall above me, manifesting through the snow, she stood tall in a sleeping gown of precious cloth, stained red with blood on her chest. She had eyes of pureness. Eyes of innocence and joy. Eyes I've only ever seen on my mother.

"M—" I couldn't utter the words, the tears welling up in my eyes.

She peered down at me, smiling softly.

"You can do this, Henry. You will do this," she said.

The wind fluttered through her hair, and it wavered softly in the dark night. Her smile glistened white as snow. Her face. . .white as snow.

"I can't," I finally said, tears streaming down my face now.

She gave me the look, the one she always gave when I had said something she knew wasn't true. Her eyebrows raised and a smirk grew across her face.

"I'm your mother, Henry," she said lightly. "I know when you are lying."

I began to pull myself up again on the side of the house.

"Help me." My voice quivered.

"I did," my mother said. Her smile never faltered, and within seconds, she took a graceful turn and disappeared into the snowstorm.

That's when I began to piece things together. The knock on the bedroom door. The door unlocking itself. It was her.

"No . . . no, Mom." I hobbled after her. As soon as my hand left the side of the cabin, I plummeted back to the ground.

My tears soaked into the crunched leaves and snow under my head. I stared blankly into the snowstorm that the ghost of my mother had disappeared into.

I began to crawl towards the front porch, pulling myself slowly by grasping onto any root or tree stump I could find nestled under the thick layer of snow and paper-thin, dead leaves. The blood on my hands stained the snow a dull crimson. With the moon setting behind the mountains, I knew I was running out of time. Within a few moments, I could nearly reach the first step.

I barely scraped the stair with the tips of my fingernails. With newfound courage, I used the step as a support to pull myself from the ground, and with a loud grunt and a shockwave of pain through my abdomen, I was off the ground. As I looked back at my path of deep red, I thought I had caught a second glimpse of my mother. Maybe she was still watching.

I quickly forced myself to the door. I placed my bloody hand on the door knob and twisted. I cautiously entered the cabin again. The place had been ransacked from where my father must have looked for me. The couch was overturned, the lanterns and lamps on the floor, my bedroom door unlocked.

And there it was. The basement door, wide open. Open like the entrance to an ominous cave. I crept toward it, watching carefully for anything to appear from the stretching darkness. I had made my way up to it and peered down.

I could see nothing.

"Father?" I yelled down the stairs.

I blindly rubbed around and felt the outline of a metal box with a switch, and I flicked it immediately. With a flash of sparks and a low hum of electricity coursing through the old wires, I began to stumble down the steep flight of stairs.

All I could hear was the taunting hum of the lights.

SLAM! A car door banged shut outside. It was Dad. It had to be. I was halfway down the stairs and swung myself around. The Shadow Man stood in the doorway.

"Keep walking," his voice echoed.

As much as I wanted my Dad to help me, I turned around and began to trek back down the stairs. Limping and wincing in pain with every step, I could barely travel down two stairs before taking a break to breathe.

"Henry!" Dad called from outside. I could hear the urgency in his voice.

I stepped down another stair. Only three more left.

"Hurry up." The whispers were back.

A shove on my back sent me tumbling down the stairs and onto the cold concrete floor. Slowly, I pushed myself up with what little strength I had left. I could faintly hear my father yelling from outside. I looked around the room, the florescent light illuminating a collection of Polaroids delicately hung by red string around the room. I counted twenty-five.

I hobbled around the room, examining each of them. As I grabbed on to every single photo, I could hear the whispers again. "Me," they would say.

"He hurt me, Henry." A sweet voice said as I grabbed a picture of a little girl.

"He's not what you think he is. . ." the familiar voice of the Shadow Man echoed.

"He's a killer, kid." Another gruff voice said as I held a picture of an older man in a rocking chair.

I made my way through the maze of pictures and souls my father had somehow affected in his lifetime. At the end of the long room was one, sole picture. I stumbled to it, placed my hand on it, and heard the voice.

"It's me, Henry" My mother's voice echoed through the room.

I stared at the picture. In it, she was standing with my father, holding me as a baby in front of the cabin. A happy family. A soon to be broken family.

"Henry?" I heard from upstairs. My father was getting closer.

I had to get out, but I couldn't let him see me. What would he do to me if he found me? Would he kill me? I couldn't take the chance. I looked up to see a hatch above me with big black letters printed across:

ESCAPE

• • •

DAVID

I wanted nothing more than to see my son's face lying asleep in his bedroom. Peaceful.

Yet I came home to emptiness. No son, doors wide open, my picture room door agape for the world to see. *He's gone,* I think to myself. I dropped to my knees, not able to find the strength to search in the forest.

The picture, Deputy Britton, the car crash. It was all for a reason. It was a reminder of the things I had done in my life that I am ashamed of. I finally released the words out of my mouth: "I'm sorry."

What I said wasn't to any particular person. It was to everyone. Everyone that I had wronged in my life before the cabin. The one person who I had wronged during life at the cabin. All of them.

I buried my head in my hands as I heard a startling explosion behind me. I looked up, and saw the flames from the fireplace lash out and surround me quicker than I had ever seen fire move before.

I stood up and attempted to make my escape.

• • •

HENRY

I pushed the hatch open, and after all the bizarre events, I almost expected a new dimension to be on the other side. Dirt and leaves fell through the cracks and the smell of fresh pine filled my nose. Then I caught a second whiff of something else, something that made my nose burn.

Smoke.

From the underground bunker I still sat in, I could see the light of fire dancing across the trees. I pulled myself up, my ribs screeching in pain, and laid on a blanket of snow. From my position, I was barely able to move my head to see the cabin. I could see through the small windows on the front porch.

Blinding red and orange flames paraded around the inside, destroying everything it touched. I tried to pull myself up but couldn't find the strength to do it. It was over now, the haven was no longer viable, the souls would be at rest.

With another strong push, I was able to force myself to the nearest tree. I sat with my back resting on it. The cabin slowly burning away from the violent slashes of heat.

Yell, Henry. Yell louder than you've ever yelled, I thought to myself. With a deep breath, I mustered up what little voice I had left.

Nothing. My voice was empty. All that could be heard was the crackling sound of the breath on my dry tongue. Something had taken my voice. I tried to scream again; they needed to hear me.

"Don't scream, Henry. You don't need to," said the sweet voice of my mother.

I turned around as quick as I could, pain shooting up my side. There she stood, cascading over me like a guardian angel. I could see others behind her now, uniformly standing in a line together.

"It's time for us to move on," she said to me, smiling, a tear rolling down her face.

"Please don't go," I said, feeling the bottoms of my eyes beginning to become damp.

"It's not a choice. I am fulfilled." She stared back at the shadows behind her.

I looked at them, too. They all stood tranquilly watching the burning cabin.

"We are fulfilled," she said softly.

With that, they all began to float over top of me, heading straight towards the cabin.

"Wait," I said. "W——" My voice was stolen once again. Given to me, and taken.

For the last time, my mother turned to me. She smiled as the tears on her face became more visible.

"I love you, Henry." I could hear a quiver in her voice. She turned back and glided towards the house.

As I watched her, I saw my father though the window. He searched frantically around the house for an escape.

As each ghost entered the cabin, the flames became bigger and more violent. The wooden walls began to split, the glass cracked. I could see my father on the inside, still hunting for his lost son.

"Come out, Dad," I yelled, my voice now returning to me.

The flames spread to the outside of the house, the front porch engulfed.

"No. No," I said to myself.

Frantically, I moved from the tree and began to crawl.

"Dad!" I yelled from the top of my lungs, begging for him to come outside.

Without acknowledgment, he kept up his search. I could tell he was losing air. I was closer now, close enough for another good yell. The front of the house was now completely covered in red and orange.

"DAD!" With a final screech, I caught his ear.

I could see through the window. My father gazed out, and we caught each other's eyes. He waved the smoke from his face as I crawled closer.

Even after all of this, a father is a father, and I needed him.

I looked up one last time to make sure he was coming out, but he was frozen, staring out the window. I could faintly see something behind him.

Mother.

He saw her reflection in the window. The foggy silhouette of my mother's spirit rose behind him. He turned around quickly, and they eyed one another as the flames crept closer to him, snaking higher and higher for what felt like an eternity.

"Come out!" I yelled again.

Nothing. They both remained, watching each other blankly. My dad's mouth was wide open as if he wanted to scream but couldn't push out any noise. My mother had a face of stone, staring down at him as she floated.

With a loud snap, the supports of the roof cracked, and the roof of the porch collapsed, blocking the front door. It didn't matter what my father did now.

I could do nothing but watch.

SNAP!

The entire roof caved in on itself, the fire engulfing the entire wooden pile almost immediately. He was gone.

Really gone.

I lay alone on the snow, tears trickling down my face. I could hear approaching sirens in the distance.

From my spot on the ground, I began to think, the smoke clouding my vision and making me lightheaded.

I drifted into a dark oblivion, watching the spirit's haven drift into it with me.

DENVER MUNCEY is a student from East Tennessee who has had a passion for storytelling since before he could even write. He would sit on his mother's lap, having her write the words he wanted over the pictures he drew beforehand. Now, he feels a bit more capable with his skills, and plans on attending college for Dramatic Writing.

NEIGHBORS

PATRICK BRIAN COOLEY

Aislinn stood in the kitchen, letting her tears fall into the sink with a hollow, metallic sound.

She awoke from a dream, disoriented in the familiar room she shared with her husband, Vaughn. This wasn't the first time; it happened years ago, before she learned not to share pillows with strangers or loved ones. Her sister—who she returned from visiting the previous day—kept a spare pillow on the highest shelf in the linen closet. "Aunt Ash's Special Pillow," her nieces and nephew called it.

And so, as she stood there over the sink in the faint,

blue light of early morning, she knew. There was only one explanation for why she would wake from another woman's dream.

• • •

Vaughn entered the kitchen a few hours later, the leaded footfall of a man with unearned confidence. Spread before him on the table were platters of biscuits, fried bologna, scrambled eggs, potato hash, and a steaming pitcher of pepper gravy.

"What's all this for?" he asked, eyebrow hooked at his wife. She was still dressed in her nightgown and slippers.

"Well," she said, shrugging one shoulder, "I've been down in Spartanburg for over a week, visiting my sister. I figured it might be nice to make my husband a hearty, home-cooked breakfast."

"Hearty? Shew, how many husbands you got, woman?" he said, bellying up to the table.

As Vaughn ate, Aislinn busied herself cleaning up the dishes. She didn't care to watch her husband eat; all he reminded her of now was a freshly slopped pig.

"Did any of the guys come over while I was gone?" she said with a strained casualness she was sure would give her away.

"Does it look like any of the guys came over?"

"I dunno," she pressed, "Jimmy is pretty good about

cleaning up after himself. I just thought—"

"What's that supposed to mean?" Vaughn sneered, "*Jimmy's* good about cleaning up after himself."

"Nothing, just—he could have been here and I'd never have known it."

After an unbearable silence, he answered, "Well you thought wrong. None of the guys stopped by, not even your boyfriend, Jimmy."

She flinched at the accusation, gripping the kitchen counter like a vice to keep from falling over from the sheer weight of his hypocrisy.

After eating his fill, she fixed him a couple egg and bologna biscuits with two, fat slices of American cheese each for his lunch; he gave her a kiss on his way out the door, to which she offered a cool, smooth cheek. As the screen door banged shut behind her husband, Aislinn dug the corner of her thumbnail into tender flesh, drawing a thin line along the semi-circumference of her forearm, over and over, until a thin red line of blood beaded up.

The following morning played out much the same, with Aislinn making a large breakfast and her husband skirting her calculatedly innocent questions. Before Vaughn was backed out of the driveway, another line marked her arm.

On the third morning, Aislinn sat down at the table with a small bowl of fruit and some black coffee after serving her husband.

"Vaughn," she said, clutching the coffee mug with

both hands.

"What?" her husband said, sighing around a mouthful of half-chewed biscuit.

"Do you love me?" Aislinn stared at her own warped reflection in the hot, black sludge. The silence hung about them, threatening to choke out all the air in the room.

Vaughn threw his fork down onto his plate with a loud clatter—a levy breaking.

"What the hell kind of question is that?" he said, flecks of egg and spittle splattering the table.

"I just—"

"You just what?" He challenged, "You just thought I'd put up with your ass out of the goodness of my heart, or. . .?"

"No," she replied, still staring into her coffee.

"Then what? It ain't your looks that keep me around, or your cooking, for that matter." He gave his plate a shove.

Aislinn closed her eyes and pressed her back into the chair, "We've just—it's different, lately. We used to talk, you used to take me out. It's been almost a year since we've even been to the movies."

"Movies? So that's it, I don't pamper you enough?"

"No, I—"

"So I must not love you because I'm too exhausted after working down at the garage all day, to put food on the table, that you burn!" He emphasized his point by flipping the plate of fried bologna over onto the table. "You are some piece of work, y'know that?"

"What?" Aislinn snapped, a knee jerk reaction she immediately regretted. Responding would only fuel his momentum; he had to be allowed to tire himself out.

"You are! Don't deny it, look at you!" He said, "Sitting there in your frumpy nightgown, serving me rubbery eggs and dry biscuits, acting like you're doing me a favor? With those new scars on your arm, to boot."

Aislinn gently tugged at her sleeve.

"Did you think I didn't notice your latest little cry for attention. You are so self-centered, sometimes I do wonder how I could have loved you. Maybe stop wasting time wondering if I love you and start thinking about what you can do to *make* me love you." With that, he pushed himself up from the table, grabbed his coat and headed for the door, tossing an, "I'm gonna be late," over his shoulder before slamming it shut behind him.

Aislinn sat in the wreckage, quivering as she carved a third and final line into her arm.

• • •

Stars were already beginning to appear along the eastern edge of the sky by the time Vaughn's pickup chugged its way up the gravel path and into their drive. Perched at the window, Aislinn peaked through a natural warp along the edge of the heavy curtains. From this vantage, she could see Vaughn as he cut off the engine and slumped over the steering wheel.

They hung there, unmoving yet intertwined until the stars worked their way nearly halfway across the sky. Finally, Vaughn raised his head and with a heaving sigh slung himself out of the cab. Aislinn flung herself onto the couch opposite their front door, as if she'd been sitting there reading *The Women's Journal* all day. She looked at him as he came in, chin tucked into her shoulder, expectant and unsure.

On the strip of floor separating the kitchen table from the living room, she had set up a simple workspace: a step-ladder with removable seat, atop which Aislinn had set a towel and scissors, with a sheet spread beneath. Absently, Vaughn ran his fingers along the side of his head, where his hair was starting to curl over the seam of his ball-cap.

"I thought," Aislinn said, teetering on a knife's edge. "It's fine. We don't have to." She moved forward, intent on clearing away the clutter.

"No." Vaughn caught her arm, freezing her beneath the tips of his fingers. "I could use a trim." Tossing his cap into the Rent-to-Own recliner, he handed Aislinn the towel and scissors and took a seat. Taking them gingerly in her arms, she secured the towel around his shoulders with a clothes pin and set to work, both of them falling into a familiar rhythm.

"Remember, not too short on top. Just enough to take

the curl out," he said.

"I know." She shook her head. "I've been cutting your hair since before we were married."

"Yeah, but sometimes you catch a wild hair up your butt and decide to try something from one of those magazines. Like the time you thought I'd look cute with 'Bieber hair' flopping down in my eyes."

"You did look cute," she insisted, a smile just touching the edges of her lips.

"Psh, I spent that whole Independence weekend at the creek blowing hair outta my eyes, the guys all giving me shit. Then they got the bright idea to steal some of your barrettes and put 'em in my hair while I was passed out."

Aislinn chuckled softly.

"What?" Vaughn asked.

"Nothing, nothing," Aislinn said.

"No, what? Something's got you all bubbling over," he grinned.

"Well, it's just," she tilted her head, touching shoulder to ear, "'steal' isn't exactly accurate. I may have sorta put them up to it." A silence bloomed, and for a heartbeat Aislinn feared she took it too far until Vaughn let out a peal of laughter, a sound she had almost forgotten and was quickly swept up in.

"Oh, woman," he sighed through a laugh, "you can be a bitch sometimes, but I love you."

The words curdled in her ears, her body suddenly tense and still. He shook his head slightly, a rolling aftershock of laughter, and she caught the edge of his ear, nicking it with the tip of the shears.

"Ow, dammit! Watch what you're fucking doing. Jesus Christ!"

"Sorry," she said, retrieving a cotton ball from the bathroom to dab away the blood. "You need to hold still now. I'm almost done." Slipping the cotton ball into her pocket, she finished up in silence. "There, go grab a shower to rinse those clippings out before you get itchy, and I'll sweep up in here before dinner."

"I already ate," he said, gingerly fingering his ear. "I'm just gonna hop in the shower and head to bed."

"Whatever you think's best."

• • •

Aislinn lay in bed, imagining shapes in the popcorn ceiling while Vaughn snored softly on his side, turned away from her. The silvery-white light of the full moon filtered through a narrow slit in the bedroom curtains, cutting a sharp line out the door and into the kitchen. Delicately, she lifted the blankets and tip-toed out of the room, shutting the door softly behind her. In the moonlit kitchen, she set to work collecting her supplies before sliding noiselessly into the night.

In the shadows, Aislinn found the familiar path, camouflaged by disuse—a secret passed down to her by her mother, and her mother's mother before her. She wound her way into the woods through thickening fog. Barefoot and resolute, she ticked off landmarks (both man-made and natural) until after nearly an hour of walking, she came to a clearing where even the mist refused to enter.

In the center stood a squat, broad stump within a circle of brown and white mushrooms. At the northern edge of the clearing, near the footpath's mouth, stood a thick, aged oak from which a heavy, iron chain caked with rust sprouted like an errant root; the iron, secured around the oak generations ago, had over the years been swallowed whole. Hoisting the chain, she wrapped it snuggly about her waist, tucked the basket under one arm, and strode into the circle.

The air stilled; not even the faint beat of a moth's wing stirred the air. In her ears, only the sound of blood pumping, steady and thunderous. Kneeling against the stump, she set her basket on the ground and began arranging things. First, a small saucer and bowl were placed in the center, to which she poured a portion of cream, and to the cream she added the blood-stained cotton ball; on the saucer, she placed a broken bit of comb generously seeping honey and stirred in a bit of hair clippings.

Head bowed, she rose and backed out of the circle, careful not to crush any of the mushrooms beneath her feet. The sounds of the night crashed in on top of her, and she nearly slipped. With her palms pressed flat against her ears, she breathed, gradually releasing the pressure. Loosing herself from the rusted chain, she coiled it back at the base of the tree, and sprinted into the fog, as if to outrun the wind.

• • •

By the time Aislinn got back to the house, the eastern horizon was a full shade lighter than the west. Later, she woke to the slamming of the front door and the cantankerous old engine turning over with a fight.

Vaughn, she thought, before rolling over and tucking her head under the covers.

By the time Vaughn returned home, however, the house was clean and a beautiful pot-roast with thick cut carrots and quartered potatoes sat keeping warm in the oven.

Aislinn had washed and primped herself, too. Her hair was pulled up, away from her face into a fishtail braid cascading over one shoulder, and she donned a light sun dress she had previously wore on their first anniversary—an ill-conceived trip to the lake that left her with a broken foot.

Vaughn paused in the doorway, eyeing his wife.

"Well, don't just stand there like a stranger," Aislinn said. "Wash your hands and pull up a seat while I get you a beer." Without waiting for a response, she whirled about and pulled two bottles from the fridge and set them on the counter.

Vaughn kicked off his boots and edged towards the sink, washing his hands before taking a seat at the dinner table. When Aislinn turned around, she was carrying a glass mug full to the brim with a frothy, domestic pale ale in each hand. Sliding Vaughn's in front of him, she took a seat catty-corner at the table.

"What's gotten into you?" he said, his beer half raised, before taking a swig.

Aislinn shrugged, "I slept in this morning, thought it would be nice for you to have a warm meal when you got home." She began nursing her beer.

"Mm-hm."

"Why don't I fix you a plate?" Without waiting for a response, she whipped the roast out of the oven, doled out a hefty portion, and carried it back to the table, both hands gripping the plate tightly. "There you go. Tuck in."

"You aren't having any?"

"Oh, maybe later," she said, tracing the rim of her beer with one finger.

Vaughn gave a half shrug, and said, "Eh, I guess it won't kill you to miss a meal," before pouring on the salt and spearing a forkful.

Aislinn's jaw tightened and the glass between her fingers nearly groaned audibly from the strain. "So. How was your day?" she forced through a tight smile.

Vaughn began to recount his morning around mouthfuls of half-masticated roast. The habit normally would have turned her stomach, but she was focusing on a large knot in the kitchen table, nodding encouragingly when he took longer pauses. The sound of the plate scraping across the table startled her back to reality. "Another plate?"

"Nah." He shook his head and leaned back in the chair.

"How 'bout another beer?"

"I thought you didn't like when I had more than one," he said.

"Since when has that stopped you?" Aislinn immediately wished she could strike the words from the air. She froze, poised on the edge of her seat.

She could feel bile curdling in her stomach when he finally broke the tension with a full throated shot-gun of a laugh, nodding, "Yeah, fair enough."

"Why don't you go make yourself comfortable in your recliner, and I'll bring you another."

Vaughn obliged, wallowing deep into the familiar indentation of his body and flicked on a rerun of something in syndication. "Here," she said, passing the drink from behind the recliner and working her fingers into his scalp.

"Mm, that feels good," he murmured and took a sip. "Ugh, why's it taste like floor cleaner?"

"Oh, I tried a 'U-Pic-6ix' from the Ingles. This one's a seasonal brew; I think they mix spruce tips in with the hops or something. I dunno, sounded fun."

Vaughn grimaced into his suds, before downing the beer in three huge gulps. "Beer's a beer, I guess." A happy warmth spread over him, his eyes heavy and his toes and fingers tingling. "Y'knough," he slurred, "S'naught hlf, bhad." His head lolled into Aislinn's palm, and she shoved it away.

• • •

When Vaughn came to, the TV was off, the night was black as pitch, and a small, unseasonable fire was crackling in the fireplace. Also, he couldn't move.

Heaving his head downward with little grace, he saw both his wrists and ankles were bound together, respectively, with bandannas from his dresser drawer. "The hell, Aislinn. When d'ja get inta th' kink shih?"

"I dunno, Vaughn?" she said from the couch, swirling the backwash remnants of her own beer at the bottom of her glass. "When did you start letting other women sleep in our bed?"

"Wha? I didn'. You don' know what you're talkin' about, Ash. That's your damn sister is what that is, she's a—"

"I wouldn't, Vaughn. I really wouldn't, right now."

"You don't talk to me like that." His eyes bulged, and he snarled, "You don't talk to me like that!"

"Really, Vaugh? From where I'm sitting, you aren't the one to be making demands. Now," she said, firmly. "How. Long."

"You've lost your damn mind. What evidence do you even think you have?"

"You let her sleep on my pillow, Vaughn."

"What? Wha—oh, seriously? Seriously! All this over your ridiculous superstition about sharing pillows?"

"You really think I don't know the difference between my own dreams and someone else's?" she spat, clenching her teeth together to keep them from chattering—with rage or fear or something else, even she wasn't sure.

"You really think you can have someone else's dreams?" he growled, incredulity and disdain dripping like spittle from his lips.

"No," she shook her head. "No. You're not doing this to me. Not anymore."

"I'm not doing anything, you're just. . .I dunno. OCD mixed with Schitzo-freaking-phrenia! But you aren't a damn psychic and I'm not cheating!"

She leaned forward and met his gaze dead-on. Vaughn swallowed, wilting under the unfamiliar force of her stare. Rising wordlessly, she glided toward the kitchen. Vaughn resumed his struggle, but his mind was groggy and his limbs were still sedate from whatever she had laced his drink with. From under the sink she produced a plastic grocery bag and marched it over to the fire. Upending it, a lump of hair clippings was unceremoniously dumped into the flames, filling the room with an acrid aroma.

"All I ever asked was for you not to lie to me, Vaughn."

"I'm not—Aislinn," he coughed. "Just untie me. We can talk."

Still facing the fire, she shook her head. "It's too late for that now. I tried. I gave you so many chances." She ran a thumb absently along the three scabbed-over scars on her forearm. "Now. . .well, they're hungry, and they've been promised a homemade meal."

Vaughn's blood turned to ice in his veins.

"What are you on about, Aislinn? Who's been promised a meal? Ash?"

She kept her back to him as she made her way to the kitchen table, unlatching a westward facing window along the way.

"Ash. Ash! Dammit, Aislinn," his voice was frantic as he struggled to crane his neck around and peer into the kitchen behind him. "You answer me, now! ASH!"

In the kitchen, what he couldn't see was a circle of salt poured around the entire kitchen table and chairs. Pulling out a seat at the head of the table, her back still to the living room, Aislinn rested her head atop her folded arms and began to cry.

Over his shrill pleading and her sobbing, a swarming sound rose in the night, buffeting the house from the west. Vaughn's words caught in his throat, but Aislinn only cried harder, clamping her hands over her ears when the first pin-prick rapping started at the window panes, working its way around towards the open window. The unlatched window made a low creaking that reverberated just underneath the skin as it swung inward. Through the stillness between Aislinn's sobs, thousands of sharpened claws scratched along the wood, etching their way across the floor and into the firelight; a thin shadow cast into the kitchen, like a child's doll made of twigs, with too many joints, pointed ears, and a bisected pair of translucent, veined wings.

Aislinn squeezed her eyes tight.

Vaughn abandoned anything even resembling human speech, his shrieks pure animalistic terror as he thrashed his head back and forth violently, in vain. No matter how hard she pressed her hands to her ears, his screams only grew louder until gradually they turned to gurgles, gurgles to wheezing, and wheezing to a soft, wet sucking with the constant sound of dripping, ripping, shredding, and crunching.

Aislinn knew the sounds of that night would linger in her ears until the last breath left her body, just as she knew that by morning, her tears would be dry.

PATRICK BRIAN COOLEY is a storyteller, blending traditions and styles from his eclectic upbringing. Raised in the military, he was born in Kansas, and has lived as far off as Northern Italy; but the bulk of his life has been spent in the U.S. South—specifically North Carolina and Tennessee—from which much of his aesthetic influences are pulled. He currently lives in Olympia, WA, where he is pursuing his bachelor's at The Evergreen State College, having recently graduated with two associate's degrees (in English and Theatre) from Northeast State Community College in Blountville, Tennessee.

WAYWARD

AMY N. EDWARDS

1965

Aliza Westinghouse knew the moment she walked into her house that something was wrong. Her mother wasn't there to greet her like normal. She yelled, "Mom?" as she walked through the house into the empty kitchen where her mother spent most of her time.

Since her mom was always cooking, she usually had some kind of snack waiting for Aliza and her brothers after school.

Ugh! She rolled her eyes just thinking about them,

her brothers. But she couldn't get distracted; she just knew her mom had made her favorite, apple fritters. She had been with her mother the day before at the supermarket and saw the ingredients in the basket and had been dreaming about the sweet, crispy fritters since Mrs. Blevin's class during second period and that ridiculous word problem about apples.

Aliza purposely didn't wait on her brothers to walk her home today. She did not need them to walk her. Besides, she knew that they would eat most of the fritters and barely leave her the crumbs.

In fact, the idea of having her brother's escort her home sent her into a momentary rage. She was sixteen years old, for crying out loud. All her brothers ever did was brag about where they were going and what they were doing—off to college or headed to a big job, just waiting to make their mark, while their parents pushed her towards attending a secretarial school in Johnson City. But what about her? She had a mind and she could do things, too! She just wished her parents, especially her mom, though she loved her dearly, would stop pushing her to do what was expected and not what she dreamed. Aliza knew what she was capable of, and she would do much more than they ever expected.

Their neighborhood wasn't dangerous and Aliza could take care of herself, but since the Vietnam War started, it had put her parents on high alert; her mother and father always insisted her brothers be around. Apparently, "Communists were everywhere and could be anyone." They lived in a small town; if there had been a communist here, people would already know.

It wasn't like a communist was going to come to East Tennessee just to kidnap her, although she wouldn't mind if one tried; she loathed the communists for the pain they put her and her family through when her oldest brother Mason was drafted. He had been MIA for a few months now. The Army told the family that there was only a ten to fifteen percent chance that he might still be alive. The news had crushed her family and altered the way her entire household functioned. There were other people in town that had lost family to the war and everyone handled it differently, but with Mason, there was the slightest chance of hope, even if Aliza was the only one holding on to that thread.

Aliza set her books on the dining room table where she would do her homework later, but she was still pondering over where her mother was. There was no note on the counter. Her mother, Helen, always left a note, especially if she was in her beauty shop, which was in the building behind their house. Aliza walked back down the hall towards the living room and the stairs that led up to their bedrooms.

She peeked into doorways and opened her mouth to call out for her mother—or, well, anyone—when unmistakably in the kitchen, the floor creaked, followed by a *thud*. She darted back down the hall and stopped just shy of the entrance. A second creak, followed by what could only be the clattering of a knocked over chair, echoed through the empty house.

Aliza carefully walked through the kitchen toward the dining room and noticed that her books and papers were scattered all over the floor and the table. A chill shot down her spine as her heartbeat sped to a near frenzy. Had they been robbed? Had her idiot brothers snuck in through the back and played a prank?

Aliza quietly walked back into the kitchen and noticed that the cabinets were open, too. Her mother kept a lot of cookbooks in those cabinets, but that was also where she kept some of her tip money she earned while cutting hair. Any of her customers could have come in and taken her money.

Aliza pushed the thought aside—surely not. All of her mother's customers were so friendly and loved the job that Helen did.

Aliza heard another sound this time from the cellar. She froze in the middle of shutting a cabinet door. Was the person still in the house? Had they hurt her mother? After what felt like the longest minute of her life, Aliza finally gathered herself, quietly tiptoed back to the front entrance, and grabbed one of the wooden baseball bats stored next to the door. With three older brothers around, Aliza knew how to use a bat. She tightened her grip, brought the bat over her right shoulder, and slowly made her way back through the kitchen, carefully stepping over the creaky floorboards.

As she reached the bottom step and put her foot on dusty concrete floor, she looked around. The musty smell of dirt, dust, and forgotten artifacts of the Westinghouse family filled her nose. The room was lined with shelves, and she knew that there were far too many creepy- crawly things living in the dark for her to spend too long in this space.

There was only a small rectangular window that provided a small beam of sunlight and a single light-bulb that she switched on with the end of the bat. The electric sizzle of the old bulb ignited with a dull glow, bringing Aliza little comfort in the suspicious dark.

She didn't need to ask if someone was with her or not; she could feel eyes watching her. She stood at the base of the steps and leaned over the stair railing, trying to see down one of the rows of shelving her dad had built that nearly divided the room in half.

The illuminated half was empty of robbers, ghosts, and stupid brothers, but she just knew something was waiting in the darker half. Baseball bat out in front of her, she tightened her grip and her resolve, ignoring the squeaking of her sweaty hands, and took a step to peek around the wall.

A small shaft of afternoon light seemed to spotlight the figure of a huge man with his back to her. He was in a brown colored suit that appeared to be made of rough fabric and a ratty newsboy cap. He was covered in dirt that fell in little crumbles as he straightened to stand at his full height. He had to be 6'4" at least and shoulders so broad she wondered how he fit down the narrow steps to the basement. He appeared to be ducked down because he was too tall, and as he rose to full height, his head seemed to blend into the board above him.

"What are you doing in my house?" Aliza screeched out, bat held high.

The figure turned towards her. As he turned, she noticed a faint greenish light that seemed to emit from his clothes. When he looked at her, the place where his eyes would have been glowed green. He didn't have eyes, just that eerie green light.

She opened her mouth to scream but nothing came out. Her heart was racing so that she felt as if she would melt from the fear and adrenaline. He pointed his crusty finger at her and said in a booming yell that seemed as if it were caught and carried away in the wind so that Aliza only got the echo of it, "JOBE!"

Aliza turned to scramble back up the stairs only to catch sight of a shadowy movement and a puff of smoke coming from underneath the steps. Another set of glowing eyes was on her, peering from beneath her feet. Where the green-eyed thing had only light for eyes, this figure's eyes had shape with its cobalt-bluish glow. But Aliza recognized the smoke scent and without even swinging the bat, she dropped it and ran, taking the steps two at a time and hoping that they were crumbling behind her so those creatures couldn't follow.

Aliza burst back through the door and landed on the kitchen floor with a thunderous *thud* and the squeal of skin on linoleum. Ian was standing at the counter and leaned over to look at her as Jack pulled his head out of the refrigerator.

"What the hell have you been doing?" Ian jerked his head towards the mess in the dining room and the cabinet doors.

"And, why were you in the basement?" said Jack with a mouthful of something or other. He was always eating. "Mom's going to kill you."

About that time, the front door of the house flung open and their mother yelled, "You three home?"

"Yep," answered Ian.

"I need to see all three of you out here, right now." Helen Westinghouse meant business.

"Shit," said Jack, wiping his mouth on his sleeve. "What did you do, Aliza? We are all in trouble now."

As they filed out the front door, Aliza saw the baseball equipment and remembered the bat she'd left behind. It would have to stay there, even if it was her home run bat from her years playing softball. The three teenagers followed their mother around the side of the house. She stopped right next to the rectangular window that shed light into the basement. It made Aliza nervous and sweaty again.

"Ahem," Helen cleared her voice and in "universal Mom code" pointed their attention to the reason they were in trouble. "Which one of you has been smoking?"

There was a pile of cigarette butts next to the window. A hint of smoke still hung in the air.

Helen waited. It took only a few minutes before

the Westinghouse children were accusing each other of smoking and trying to explain to their mother.

"I am old enough to smoke if I want to," spouted Ian. "But I am not that stupid."

"Uhm, hello," Aliza piped in, "asthma. It would kill me."

"Fine," pouted Jack. "Pin it on the middle kid. I didn't do it though. It would mess with my baseball workouts."

Helen merely put her hand up, and everyone fell silent.

"I will not tolerate smoking in or around my house. I have clients who walk this way to get to my salon. I don't need them seeing a mess like this. I want it cleaned up, and I don't want to catch a single one of you with a cigarette, ever. I don't care what they say, that stuff will kill you."

She smiled and turned on her heel; as she walked back towards the front door, she said over her shoulder, "Supper will be ready at five-thirty. I will need help with the table at five, right Aliza?"

"Yes Ma'am," Aliza answered, rolling her eyes.

When Aliza looked back at her brothers to begin arguing who would clean up the mess, they were gone, laughing as they rounded the back of the house. She didn't know who had been smoking here but she really didn't suspect it was anyone in her family.

As she used a small gardening shovel to scoop up the mess, she knelt down and caught the scent of the tobacco. She glanced up towards the house only to find herself staring at the window to the basement. She jumped at her reflection in the glass and mumbled about her nerves. She finished cleaning up, and as she glanced back at the window, the blue glowing eyes were peeking through the window at her. She screamed and fell back about the same time her mother must have entered the kitchen.

"Aliza Jolene Westinghouse!" Her mother screeched, "Get in here right now!"

Aliza covered the cigarettes with some dirt and hurried toward her doom. Her mother was truly a loving, caring, and kind person, but Helen Westinghouse ran a tight ship. Aliza's eyes widened as she remembered that whatever supernatural event took place left quite a mess in the dining room. She closed her eyes and took a breath, just hoping her brothers had thought to shut the cabinet doors.

"Momma," started Aliza as she entered the kitchen and went toward the dining room and the mess of papers, "when I came in from school, I couldn't find you and I heard some strange noises so I went to check it out. I don't know what made this mess but it was not me. But I don't mind to pick it up."

Her mom nodded and then began helping clean things up.

"Mom," Aliza was sitting on her knees, a stack of disheveled papers in her hands. "Have you ever seen a ghost?"

She swallowed hard and felt goosebumps prickle her skin.

"A ghost?" Her mom chuckled. "How ridic——" she started to say, but then she looked at Aliza. "I mean, I suppose it is possible, Sweetheart. Listen, just because we live across from that old cemetery doesn't mean anything. Every town, including small ones like Erwin, have tall tales. Why would you ask such a thing?" It was genuine curiosity, and there was something in the look that her mother gave her that made Aliza think there was something she was hiding.

"Well, I saw something weird down in the basement a few minutes ago. Not really sure," Aliza paused. She didn't want her mom to think she was crazy.

"It was probably just the neighbor's silly cat." Her mom shook her head and dusted off her skirt as she stood. "Chester slips through the window that won't latch all the time. I heard him down there hissing one day and by the time I got down the steps to help him, the window was clunking shut again."

Helen helped her daughter stand and then pulled her into a hug. "Why don't you go lie down until supper? It seems like you have had a crazy afternoon."

"Yeah," said Aliza. "It has been a little weird."

She took her mother's advice and ran upstairs to her room. She pulled the curtains shut, kicked off her shoes, and flopped on the bed. She reached over to her nightstand to check the time and bumped the table with her hand, knocking something in the floor. The loud clunk told her immediately that it was the bat that she had abandoned in the basement. It still had dirt and dust on it from where she had dropped it, and it wasn't until then that she noticed the faint smell of cigarette smoke in the air.

Aliza remembered the first time she encountered that particular scent of smoke. When they had first moved to Erwin, ten years ago in 1955, her new classmates were always excited to tell her that her house was haunted. At first she thought they were just being silly and trying to scare the "new kid," but more than once she had seen things to make her think that maybe they were right. She had seen shadowy figures but decided it was just her imagination and thoughts brought on by the other kids' stories. But then there was "The Smoker."

She had been looking out across the street at the Jobe Cemetery. The lightning bugs were just starting to flicker and a man was standing in the graveyard, head down as if he were staring at a marker. He let out a little puff of smoke and his gaze shifted, and Aliza could have sworn he looked straight at her. But there was no way that he could have seen her; she was too far away and it was dark in her room. She pulled the curtains and went to bed. She had not been asleep for long when she woke, coughing and choking because her asthma was abruptly kicking in.

Smoke. She smelled cigarette smoke.

As she coughed and fumbled around to turn on the light, she saw the outline of the same dark figure, poof of smoke and all, standing at the side of her bed, peering down at her with faded blue light for eyes.

Her curtains, which she knew she had pulled shut, were standing open and the pale light of the moon illuminated the shadowy presence that hovered over her. She went from coughing to screaming, and by the time she got a light on, the figure was gone.

Try explaining that to the parents.

• • •

Aliza managed a nap even though the stress of what she had seen that afternoon was enough to keep her from sleeping for a few weeks. She must have been tired, or maybe she didn't want to think about all the homework she was going to have to reorganize after one of the figures threw it all over the dining room. At any rate, she slept until her mother woke her for dinner with a little shake.

"Aliza," her mother nudged her shoulder, "supper is ready. You need to get washed up."

"Wha—?" Aliza wiped the sleep from her eyes.

"Sugar," said her mom. "Supper is ready. Aliza, really, what is that old baseball bat doing up here?"

Aliza snapped to a sitting position and looked at the bat again. Her eyes went wide, but her mother didn't seem to notice. "Honey, put that thing back downstairs and hurry up. If your brothers get impatient, there may be nothing left."

Her mother left the room, and Aliza flashed back through everything that had happened that afternoon. She had not brought the bat. He had. The blue eyed one. She took the bat, returned it to its normal spot, and washed her hands on the way to the table. Everyone was already seated and grumbling that she was late.

"I'm starving," said Jack, "Sit down! Now!"

"You be nice to your sister," said Aliza's father, John. "The crumbs of your 'snack' after school trail all over the place, so you couldn't be that starved. And take that damn hat off at the table."

Aliza slid into her chair and the blessing was said. After everyone's plate was full, the sharing began. It was a custom to share some portion of their day with the family; it could be a funny story, a concern, or just any old thing. Helen spoke of one of her clients being so complimentary of her work; John informed them about some new contract that the Clinchfield Railroad line might be getting and how it could help with his promotion, which led to Jack hinting about some new baseball equipment that he would need so he could score a big scholarship or maybe go straight to the big leagues. Ian shared his plans to go to college and the kind of financial help he would need to make his dream of becoming an accountant a reality. Aliza took it all in and was the last to speak, as usual.

"Well, if Ian is going off to school, I don't see why I can't?" She didn't even take a breath to let anyone begin to argue. "I want to become a lawyer. I want to learn and know things and travel. I don't see why they get all the attention, and I only get to wish for a good marriage. I can do anything I want!"

Everyone at the table was staring at her when she finished.

"You want to what?" asked her dad. "Girls don't really go to college like that, Sweetie. Besides, once we put Ian through school and maybe Jack. . ." He left the thought hanging in the air for everyone to finish on their own. *Of course*, thought Aliza, *a college fund for the boys but nothing for the girl*. It was medieval.

"That is so unfair!" she said maybe a little louder than she had intended.

"Aliza," snapped her mother. "Do not raise your voice at this table, and definitely not to your father or to me. Would you like to finish this dinner or would you like to go to your room and contemplate being selfish and rude?"

Aliza dropped her fork in her plate with an audible *clank*. "I think I need a little time to myself," she said and marched up the steps to her room without another word. Once in her room, she paced, mumbling about how her brothers always got what they wanted and how it was like she didn't even exist sometimes. The longer she paced, the more she thought about just leaving. "Hell," she muttered, "I doubt they would miss me anyway." Her train of thought was derailed by a light knock at the door.

"Hey," said Jack quietly, one of the few times he had

ever been quiet in his life. "Aliza, come on."

Aliza snatched the door open so quickly that her brother jumped a little. *Good,* she thought. "What is it?"

"Hey," he started and took a step inside her room for privacy, "so, I know you are a little down, what with getting caught smokin' and all that at dinner, so I brought you two things. First . . ." He brought one of his hands from behind his back and produced a plate with a giant piece of chocolate cake on it. "Mom doesn't need to know that I smuggled this out of the kitchen for you." Aliza couldn't help but smile.

"What about door number two?" she said motioning toward his other hand as she took the plate.

"Ta-Da," he said as he handed her a large silver flashlight scavenged from the junk drawer (her dad called it the tool drawer) in the kitchen.

"Are you going to put on a shadow puppet show?" she laughed as she took a few steps and sat on her bed to finish the cake.

"Gah," he grumbled and rolled his eyes, "Ian and I are going to check out the cemetery across the road tonight. They say Old Dawg comes to visit a lot, and I thought you might want to come, too. Unless you are too chicken." He waved the flashlight in front of her, "Too much of a girl."

Now it was Aliza rolling her eyes. She snatched the light out of his hand and nearly dropped the last bite or two of cake off the plate balanced in her lap. "You're on. What time? How are we getting out?"

Jack told her the plan and slipped back out the door; he was even kind enough, for once, to take the plate with him. Aliza knew that something was up. He was never thoughtful like that; "dishes were for girls to worry about," after all. She opened her bedroom door just a crack so she could hear Jack talking to Ian.

"I think this is a dumb idea," said Ian, always the voice of reason. "Besides, she is going to be so pissed she may never speak to us again."

"Come on, man," said Jack. "It will be hilarious to scare her. I gave her the flashlight and everything. It's just a prank. Plus, she has to speak to us again at some point. We are her brothers after all. I mean, aren't we supposed to pick at her sometimes?"

"I don't think you understand this 'big brother' thing very well," said Ian, "but I guess since she agreed we could goof around a little."

Aliza didn't bother closing the door back; she was already too mad to care if anyone heard her. She slammed things around for a few minutes, mainly pillows, which didn't help her feel better. "Play a prank on me," she muttered to herself, "I can do better than that."

She grabbed her purse and dumped its contents on the bed. She retrieved her money from the coffee can stash in her closet and put it in her wallet. She picked out her favorite outfits and handful of personal things, stuffed them in the purse, and slipped out of her room. It was not quite dark so she wouldn't need the flashlight, and she ran across the street to the cemetery and stowed her bag behind one of the larger grave markers. "Thank you Davis family for keeping an eye on my stuff. I will be back for it later tonight."

As she was leaving the cemetery, she could have sworn she heard something. Not like a twig snap but more a voice echoing in the breeze. It sounded like a groan at first but turned into a whisper; "Here," it seemed to say in a long, wheezing breath. She looked around but didn't see anyone. There was an audible *thunk* on the tree just behind her. It was enough to send her running back to her house and the safety of her room.

As she waited in her bedroom for her brothers to retrieve her for their "fun," she looked out her window, pondering whether she would ever come back or not. It was a bit ironic that her hope seemed to lay in the cemetery, a place for the end of things was a possible new beginning for her. She looked across the way at the cemetery and saw a flicker, like the reddish glow of a cigarette mid-smoke. She squinted as if it would help her see better in the twilight, but she blinked and it was gone. It wasn't long before her brothers came to get her.

"Don't forget your flashlight," smirked Jack. "Maybe bring your baseball bat, too." He motioned towards the bat leaning against the nightstand.

"I put that downstairs a little bit ago," she said, eyes wide.

"Yeah, right," said Ian. "Can we get this show on

the road?"

"No, really, I—" stuttered Aliza.

"She's trying to chicken out," said Jack, knowing the taunt was all the encouragement that she needed.

"I. Am. Not. A. Chicken." Aliza accentuated the last word by picking up the bat and poking Jack in the chest with it.

"Fine," he said, hands in the air like she was holding a gun on him, "prove it." He turned and led the way to her window.

"What now?" she asked.

"We have to climb out your window," said Jack, like it was so obvious. "It is the lowest drop to the ground floor. Ian and I will catch you." Without waiting for her to protest, he climbed out the window and onto the short slant of roof over the front porch. He angled his feet to slide onto the porch railing and then jumped to the grass. Ian followed, and Aliza did, too. She couldn't hold on to the roof's edge long enough to swing towards the porch, so her brothers did, in fact, catch her, but nothing was said as tensions were already high.

The siblings crossed the street as the dim light of the moon showed their path. There weren't many street lights in this part of town and they didn't want anyone to see their flashlights just yet.

"Let's talk to Old Dawg," said Jack moments after walking past the first headstone in the graveyard.

"Not Old Dawg," said Ian. "I hear he is awful mean."

"Who is Old Dawg?" asked Aliza, half playing along.

"You mean you don't know?" said Ian, starting to sound like some silly radio show or something in an old Poe story. "Lots of people say he isn't real, but lots more say he killed twenty something people right in this cemetery, stabbed them with a big ol' knife. But, it wasn't always a cemetery; it used to be the place all the hoboes would hide and drink and gamble and whatever else hoboes did. The track runs down behind those bushes you see," he pointed towards the back of the cemetery. "They say Old Dawg used to run a gambling ring until one night he cheated some fool out of all his money and that feller waited until Dawg was standing around, counting his money, and someone came up behind him, took his own knife and slit his throat. They say in Old Dawg's final breath that he swore he would use the same knife that killed him to gut anyone who came into his territory again. Guess where we are standing?"

Aliza knew the answer without saying it. She glanced around expecting to see the blue glowing eyes peering at her from behind a gravestone, but there was nothing. She and her brothers walked around for a while; she stayed close for a few minutes, letting them think she was actually scared. Truth be told, she was scared.

Aliza heard Ian inhale sharply, and when she flipped her flashlight towards him, he was pointing at a rusty old knife stuck in the ground next to a tree. She heard Jack approaching behind her and turned to glare at him, but it wasn't Jack. It was the green-eyed figure she had seen in the basement. She choked on a scream and took a step back, stumbling over a headstone. Her head slammed onto the ground and the next thing she saw was Ian holding the flashlight under his chin, making stupid faces.

"Dang Aliza," he said, "watch where you are going."

"Are you okay?" continued Ian. "It sounded like a hard fall. What scared you? And don't say Jack, I know it wasn't him."

"I thought," she said rubbing the lump forming on the back of her head, "I saw something. I guess I am a little spooked." She shook it off and started walking again.

She was near the Davis headstone that hid her secret when there was a rustle in the bushes down next to the railroad tracks that ran along the back of the cemetery. Her attention snapped towards the noise, and she heard a sharp rumbling sound—a growl and yell mixed together.

"What was that?" asked Ian into the dark. "Old Dawg," he whistled like he was calling a dog, "Old Dawwwgggg. Come here boy."

The wind kicked up with Ian's taunt; the rustling and growling got louder, but it was not like any animal Aliza had ever heard before. Ian edged closer to the rustling bushes, expecting Jack to pop out, per the plan, but as Ian's flashlight moved to light the bushes, he realized Jack was suddenly behind him and Aliza.

So, what had he been provoking?

No sooner had the three siblings had this thought when a burly, lumbering figure, barreled out of the bushes, growling more ferociously than a grizzly bear. Jack and Ian both dropped their lights and ran towards the house. Aliza was too stunned to move. The boys reached the house and were hunched over in the shadows to catch their breath when they realized that Aliza wasn't with them.

"Shit, did we leave her in the cemetery?" Ian huffed.

"Yep," said Jack. "I ain't going back in the place. If she didn't have the sense to run. . ."

"Dammit, Jack," said Ian. "We can't leave her over there." It took them a moment but they mustered the courage to go back for their sister.

Meanwhile, Aliza gawked straight at the figure stalking slowly towards her and realized it wasn't a bear, but a man. The man stepped into the beams of the dropped flashlights, revealing a brown suit. While his body was in the light, his face remained in the shadows.

"Uhh. . .hello?" said Aliza, her voice shaking. "Thanks for scaring off my stupid brothers." It wasn't too far of a stretch to think it was a passerby or maybe even a random hobo. They still passed through here from time to time, right?

"I hear brothers can be a pain like that," said the man in a smooth voice. "Never had one I could speak of. Would you like to get even with them?" He sounded like a salesman starting his pitch.

"I guess," she muttered, realizing she was close enough to the Davis headstone and reached for her bag, hoping that maybe she could make a run for it.

Not taking her eyes off the man in the shadows, she swung the bag over her head so the strap hung across her body. "I would love to get even. I am tired of always being treated second. They get all the attention and they get to go to college; apparently boys can do anything they want but girls aren't allowed. I have the ability to do all the things they can, but I never get to just because I am the girl, the little sister. It is so damn frustrating! No, it is infuriating!"

Alize saw Ian and Jack in their yard, waving her to come back to the house. They had run when she didn't, huh? Boys.

"Well, Little Lady, all you have to do is go over there and pick up my knife," said the figure; his voice was hypnotizing. "At big one next to that tree over yonder." He jerked his chin in the direction, and as his head moved Aliza noticed the green glow that flashed where his eyes should have been. She gasped in fear and recognition but immediately dismissed it as the voice lulled her into submission. "Get that knife, and I can help ya."

She nodded as if she were settling into a trance and her feet shuffled in the direction he motioned. She bent down and peered at the rusty bladed Bowie knife left too long in the elements.

"That's it," said the velvety voice. "Now pick it up and go kill them brothers of yours for being bastards."

"Yeah, that will teach them," she muttered. She looked up to see the boys headed across the street. They were at the edge of the cemetery, coming back to stir up more trouble. Did they think they could scare her? *Oh,* she thought, even though she wasn't sure it was entirely her thought, *I will show them. I will scare the shit out of them, and then I will finish them.*

Aliza was inches from the blade; she could smell the damp earth, and she swore she could taste the copper tang of blood as the image blinked in and out of her mind: the blade in her hand and her brothers bloodied in front of her. She took a breath, her hand starting to curl around the handle, when she heard a different voice, "Aliza, I'm over here."

Aliza blinked and shook her head as the hold of the shadow man's suggestions shattered. She looked in the direction from which the voice came and saw the smolder of the cigarette and blue eyes glowing back at her.

"Hey!" She stood up, leaving the knife in its place. Aliza stalked angrily towards the new fellow, "Are you following me? What do you want from me?"

"Wait a second, Darlin'," said the smooth shadow voice, "I thought we were getting even with your brothers. That's what you really want, isn't it? Leave Old Smoky over there alone. I am the one who can help you get the respect you want."

"Shut up, Leo, and let the girl alone," said the man with the cigarette. "She knows better. She knows killin' her brothers ain't gonna help her situation. Why don't you go back to Hell where you belong?"

At that, the man in the shadows took a step closer, facing her. Aliza flicked the beam of her flashlight towards him, and he flinched; it was green-eyed ghost from her basement. She screamed and nearly dropped the light as she stumbled backwards. He stomped towards her, and she realized she didn't know how to fight a ghost. She could feel the anger, the evil, and the desire to kill pouring from him in waves. She could not believe that only moments ago he had nearly compelled her to kill her brothers. She looked around to see if Ian and Jack were coming, but they had disappeared. Had they really abandoned her?

The man with the cigarette stepped between her and the green-eyed thing.

"Leo, I keep telling you," said the protective figure. "This is my place, I will always win. That is how good and evil works."

"Oh," growled Leo, "I will show you what evil is." He dove at the slim figure standing in front of Aliza. She screamed, not knowing what to expect.

The two men, or ghosts—she wasn't even sure what they were at this point—rolled around, knocking each other into, no, through headstones. A punch was thrown here and there, and the next thing she knew, the rusty blade had replaced the cigarette in the slim man's hand. Leo let go of the other man's collar.

"You don't have the guts," said Leo, but he was clearly afraid that he was wrong.

"We have been down this road before," said the man as he stood up. "You were the murderer; I was the victim. Now that we are like this, I can do whatever I like to punish you and protect her. That's how it works. Remember? So, the question is, do you want me to stab you with your own blade and you disappear for a while or do you want to leave on your own?"

"Damn you, Jobe!" Leo ran at Jobe in an attempt to tackle him and start the fight once more. Jobe was holding the knife with both hands and raised it above his head. As Leo crashed into him, he brought the knife down into Leo's back. Leo groaned and slumped away as green and black shadows oozed out of the wound. "One day," gasped Leo. "One day I will take you with me to Hell!" The shadows that had oozed out of him seemed to wrap around him, and in a moment he was gone.

Aliza stood there, frozen. What the hell had she just witnessed? How was she supposed to breathe, much less move?

As the shadows consumed Leo, he had let out miserable screams and threats. She knew he would be back, and she wasn't about to be there when he did. Aliza had edged her way towards the rails; she glanced back one more time and ducked behind some bushes and began running. She ran for what seemed like forever before she slowed because of her wheezing. Damn her stupid asthma.

She looked around in an attempt to figure out where she was. Things appeared very different than the streets. She had made it as far as Fishery Park, at least that is where she thought she was. Her flashlight barely made a dent in the darkness.

After she caught her breath, she began walking slowly, the crunch of the gravel around the crossties did not drown out the snap of a twig in the woods or the creepy hoot of an owl before it dove after its prey. She was just glad she hadn't encountered a train yet. She didn't relish diving into the tangled woods nearby.

Her light caught the edge of a clearing and she sped up, thankful for a grassy area and a part of the park that was familiar. She flopped down in a heap on the damp grass and tried to collect her thoughts. "What the hell have I done?" she asked herself out loud.

She took a deep breath and smelled the damp night air, the tar of the crossties, and the all-too-familiar pungent odor of cigarette smoke.

Aliza saw the pale bluish form leaning against a tree at the edge of the clearing. "What do you want from me?" she cried, fear and tears in her voice as she stood and took some stumbling steps backwards.

He didn't answer; instead he asked, "I see you have a bag there. Where you headed?"

She forgot she was running away for a second. After all, it had been a scary, crazy night.

"I am going that way down the tracks," she started. "I—I am not even sure what just happened, but I don't want to be a part of your or that other guy's problems. That guy, Leo, he was talking to me in this crazy smooth voice, and I couldn't resist what he was saying. He wanted me to kill my brothers with some old knife. And my brothers, they knew I was having a tough day and what did they do? Play a prank! I heard them planning it. I'm tired of playing second fiddle to my brothers."

She stopped for a second and flashed to the idea of the bloody knife and her brothers stabbed to death. How could she even have thought those things? It brought her back to the moment. "Sorry," she muttered, "I tend to ramble when I get. . ."

"Mind if I walk with you a piece?" said the blue man's voice. "I am Jobe. If you will let me, I will explain it all—well, as much as I can."

"How do I know I can trust you?" Aliza asked with genuine concern. "I mean you and that burly, scary dude, Leo, just fought and tried to get me to kill my brothers and . . ." Realization set in, "You are that shady dude that is always in the cemetery. You—came into my room and—you were in my basement today! And holy shit! Are you the reason I had to clean up cigarette butts today? Thanks a million for that, Buddy." She began pacing in anger, eventually rambling herself into a calm before she turned to face the man who called himself Jobe.

"Well, I can answer most of those questions but only if you agree to let me walk with you a bit," he said. "I think I might be able to help you with your story if you listen to mine. It's kind of what I do." He smiled and flicked the cigarette into the gravel. "As for trusting me, I did prevent Leo from getting his way and makin' you kill them brothers of yours. All you have got to do if you get to feeling afraid of me is pray for me to leave."

Aliza huffed her disbelief.

"What?" said Jobe. "Don't you believe in praying?"

"Well," she said, quieter, "I did but then my brother went off to Vietnam. I prayed and prayed but they can't—no, they won't tell us what happened to him, whether he is dead or alive. It is so hard—" She paused to try to hold back the tears and keep herself together.

"I reckon that would cause a lot of hurt," responded Jobe. "I am not sure my daddy ever really forgave me for running off but—" He hesitated.

"Yeah, I ran off just like you and roamed the rails for a few years," said Jobe. "I had a stupid fight with my Dad, and I just left." He puffed on a new cigarette that she didn't even see him light. "Well, I came home once, but it didn't go too well. I couldn't understand how he could be so close-minded. I mean, we talked about responsibility and the like, but I didn't want to be a part of that family anymore. Instead I found a new family, some people call us bums, hobos, drifters, beggars, vagabonds, but hidden in all those names are people in situations doing the best they can."

"I get it," said Aliza. "Family is not always what it is cracked up to be."

"Now, hang on," said Jobe, "I just meant you can find family in some interesting places."

Jobe had already started walking as they talked and Aliza was intrigued enough to follow along. They ambled slowly through the darkness; a hint of moonlight hit the rails from time to time and the bugs resumed their noises as Jobe and Aliza's voices seemed to easily blend in to the cacophony.

"So, you ran away from home, too?" asked Aliza as she bit at her thumbnail, still a little unsure about this Jobe fellow.

"Well, the first time I didn't," he began. "The first time I just wanted to see what it was like. I lived over in Johnson City and saw these fellers riding the rails all the time. I liked the idea that even though they didn't have hardly anything to their names, they could still see the world, you know wind in their hair and such. So, I tried it."

"You jumped a train out of Johnson City?" said Aliza, skeptical. "Just like that."

"Nooooo," he shook his head. "It was not easy at all. I just about didn't make it onto the car. If this guy named Ray hadn't helped me, I would never have made it on that first jump or my first ramble on the rails. You know, people don't always think about how they are going to get a bite to eat or a place to sleep when they jump the rails. Well, I didn't at least, and Ray took care of me."

Jobe paused for a moment as if considering how to explain himself. As they continued, they walked into a bit of a fog, and then it was like watching a film on the big screen; the fog was the screen and Jobe was projecting his memory.

..

Come on," said Ray as he pulled Jobe up a rickety set of steps behind him. They had climbed up the steep bank and partial wall from the train yard in Erwin and slipped between the post office and the YMCA building—a place where they were allowed to sleep when it was cold out. Ray pulled Jobe in the direction of a two story brick building near the corner of one of the streets. The bottom level was a small grocery store, but the top level was their apparent destination.

"I have heard that this lady is good to our kind," Ray ran his fingers through his hair, smoothing down the dirt of who knows how many days without a bath. He dusted off his clothes and tried to look presentable. Jobe saw and copied him. "Ol' Frank, the one that travels as a carny sometimes said she is a fine cook."

"I don't feel too good about this, Ray," Jobe said, always glancing around, expecting someone to judge or chase them away. Asking for help always left a bad taste in his mouth, but then again, he hadn't eaten a real meal in so long he wasn't sure whether he was going to let his pride or paranoia get the best of him.

"Nah," chastised Ray, "just wait and see. Not everyone hates us." He knocked on the door.

A beautiful petite lady with dark brown hair and a sweet smile opened the door. "What can I do for you?" she said as her three children gathered behind her. The youngest, barely four years old, was peaking around her mother's skirts.

"Ma'am," said Ray as he took his rumpled, dirty hat off and held it at his chest. "I know times are hard, but if you had any food *you could spare, we would be mighty appreciative." He smiled and dropped his head in a little nod that was almost a bow.*

"Sir," she said, her voice soft and light but with an edge of someone not to be trifled with, "as you can see I have lots of mouths to feed and my husband, a railroader through and through, should be home any minute. I wish I could help but. . ." She didn't finish.

"Thank you anyway," said Ray as he and Jobe turned to go back down the rickety steps.

"Wait," she said, stepping just outside the door. "I wasn't finished." She sighed, "These are hard times for sure and I do have lots of mouths to feed, but I suppose a few more won't hurt too much. It won't be much but——"

"That's just fine, Ma'am. We will have what you give us." Ray smiled and took a step back from the door.

"You gentlemen sit right there on those steps for a few minutes while I cook." She introduced her kids as she tied on an apron, all of them still standing in the doorway.

'That little one there is Kay, the middle one is Stevey, and Suzy is the oldest." She smiled lovingly at her children.

Ray and Jobe sat down on the step as she pushed the door closed, but it wasn't even a minute until the kids were out the door, peppering the men with questions.

"What's it like ridin' the rails?" asked Stevey, clutching a baseball in one hand and a glove on the other. He tossed the ball into the glove and went on, "Yeah, if I don't make the major leagues and play like Babe Ruth then I might work on the railroad like my daddy or maybe ride the rails like you fellers." He smiled.

"Well," Jobe said quietly, "I don't think that riding the rails like we do is——"

Kay, who at first appeared to be shy, interrupted the beginning of the conversation to tell some crazy story about her siblings making her jump off of a roof top.

"Kay," snapped Suzy. "You ain't supposed to tell, remember?" She smacked at her sister's hand, but Kay dodged it and went on.

"But Sissy," she pointed, "it was right there." Her little finger pointed at the edge of the roof that was about six feet away from a wall at the back. Just looking at it, if a jumper missed the wall, it was a straight two-story drop to the tiny alley behind the building.

Suzy walked over and took her sister's hand to stop her pointing. She leaned down and whispered in the little girl's ear and Kay's eyes were wide with shock. "You wouldn't dare!" said Kay.

"Why'd you go and do that?" asked Stevey, clearly concerned for his younger sister. "She is just little. We shouldn't have done that anyway."

The two of them turned to Jobe and Ray, almost forgetting that the two men were there in the first place. Both kids smiled and went down the steps and across the street to play catch in the baseball field next to the YMCA.

Ray breathed a sigh of relief about the time the door opened and the kind lady, Kate, handed each of the men a plate of breakfast foods. Jobe's mouth was watering before he fully had a hold on the plate. She left them to eat and came back a moment later with two cups of coffee.

"Gentlemen," she said leaning against the railing as they ate. "Where are you two from originally?"

"Oh here and there," answered Ray, trying to not talk with food *in his mouth. "I am originally from Dante, Virginia. Lost my job in the coal mines, lost my family in them mines, too." His voice had quieted and he drifted off into his grief for a moment.*

Kate put her hand on his arm in comfort and it snapped him back. "Every time that darn fool I married goes to work, I worry whether he will come home or not. Railroad is a hard life and a dangerous one, too." She shook her head and glanced down for a moment. Then, she looked up at Jobe, waiting for his answer.

"I come from a place down in North Carolina that was too small to name," he chuckled a little. "Truly Ma'am if you blink, you'll miss it. Thank you for your kindness. That there had to be the best meal I believe I ever ate." He smiled as he handed her the plate. "Would you like me to do up my plate, Misses?"

"Nah," she shook her head, proud of her cooking and the compliment. "I will just add it to the rest. There will be plenty to do when Pete gets home." She smiled and took both the plates and coffee mugs. "You gentlemen be safe and blessed in your travels."

••

The fog dissipated, as did the memory, and Aliza was left in awe of what had just happened. She recognized the family; she would have to ask Kay about this sometime—well, if she ever returned to Erwin.

"Ray was like family to me," said Jobe. "He had lost someone he loved in the coal mines in Virginia and just left. But that little family we visited that day didn't see bums or hobos, they saw two people. Pete's family helped us out a few times after that. Good people. Families have problems and secrets and sometimes it gets hard but. . ." He looked up at Aliza and realized he was losing her, so he continued.

"After that, we rode through Erwin and on up the line. I stopped off with Ray at a little place called Lost Cove. It ain't even there anymore, but it was a little community that could only be reached by the rail. Ray had some talking to do, so I found a spot to light for a while and this little lady sat down next to me and started talking. Told me all kinds of stories about her boy, his daddy that basically sent them to live there, and how her boy had run off. She missed him something terrible and wished that he would come home." He looked up at the sky to take in the stars for a minute, as if they were fueling his story.

"And?" Aliza was impatient.

"And," he brought his focus back down to earth and turned to look at her. "I went home."

It was really the first time he had looked at her, face to face in that close of a distance, and he was surprised that she didn't jump. So much about this girl had shocked him. She seemed so unafraid of so much.

"What?" she asked almost disappointed. "You think that lame story is going to make me want to go home?" She took a step past him and sped up.

"Wait a second," he said catching up to her. "That time I went home because I needed the old man to be straight with me about what I had seen."

"A place like Lost Cove," she questioned, "what was so shocking about that?"

"I was about to tell you but you went running off in a huff," he pulled another cigarette out and lit it. "Sorry about getting you in trouble earlier. Sometimes when I am getting close to a runner, I burn through 'em."

"How is it you can even smoke?" She asked, "You are a ghost, right?"

"That I am," he said. "A bit shocked that you ain't scared and haven't been since you have been seeing me for a while now."

"I guess you don't scare me," she said trying to act tough. "So far, you haven't really given me much reason to. Well, other than looming over me in my room. You protected me in the cemetery and returned my bat. But that other guy that you fought with, he was scary. What was his problem?"

"Leo," puffed Jobe. "Leo has a lot to be bitter about. He always hated me, but I didn't really know why. We are kinda stuck together because we, well. . ." He hesitated.

"We. . .what?" asked Aliza, maybe sounding a little like an annoyed teen.

"Have you ever heard any railroad tales?" he asked. "Ghosts like us and all?"

"I have heard of Old Dawg," she said. "Stupid stories from the kids at school and my idiot brothers."

"Anything else?" he asked. "Actually, just let me

show you something else. It may explain a few things."

He puffed some smoke, and just as before Jobe's memories spilled into the night.

• •

The sickly crack of the club to the back of his skull told Jobe that it was all over. Jobe's vision slipped in and out of darkness as he slid slowly to the ground. His head bounced once and the railroad police bull stepped over his body.

"Damn worthless hobos," spewed the railroad bull. "Old Dawg really must have it in for you, Buddy. Told me to rough you up special and he would owe me one. Got him a brand new knife for snitching on you bastards. Might just have to have him use it on a few of your buddies." The club rose to smack him again but Jobe blinked one last time and darkness took him.

Jobe woke a few hours later with one of the nastiest headaches he had ever had. He looked up and saw Ray, who must have dragged him away from the spot the bull had left him.

"Damn that Old Dawg!" Jobe said bending his arm across his eyes to keep out the painful light of being awake. He touched the back of his head to find dried blood and a baseball-sized lump. "Thought I was a goner. Thanks for gettin' me outta there."

"What do you mean? It wasn't him that hit you," said Ray. "You're welcome by the way. Honestly, what would you do without me, Jobe?"

"It wasn't him that hit me but it was him that caused it. You *know he turns us in to the bulls. He seems to always want me out of the picture the moment I arrive," said Jobe, pulling his slender form to a more upright position, an action he instantly regretted.*

"Ugh!" he muttered as he set his old fedora on his head and pulled the brim low over his eyes. "I will get that old bastard."

"Yeah," said Ray, getting riled up. "You should have heard old Frank the other day. Said Old Dawg was keepin' an eye on places, you know families and the like that help us. Said he pushed one of Kate and Pete's kids down the last few steps next to the grocery. Pete caught her though and Dawg got beat down. That Pete used to box, and he's built like a rock." He laughed a little, "I wish I could have seen that. Frank said Pete damn near knocked Dawg's teeth out. Told him if he ever saw him or heard of him anywhere near his family he would come back and finish him off."

"Good for Pete!" Jobe said, meaning it. "Someone should do something about that good for nothing. Reckon I need to get out of here for a while. I need the wind in my face and Erwin at my back."

"Don't go hatin' on Erwin," said Ray, standing and reaching to help his friend to his feet.

"I ain't hatin' on Erwin, lot of good people around here. But that old bastard has the bulls on high alert," said Jobe with a pained smile. "Let's go."

"I'll walk you down to the yard but I am going to stick around for a little while. Word on the street is there may be a job or two open at the pottery, and I will do about anything to stay put for a while," said Ray.

"What?" asked Jobe, shaking his head, "I thought you loved riding the rails."

"I used to love it, but I—" he stumbled over the words, "I—I

kind of have met someone and I want to see where that goes. I had a life once, what people would have called normal. I have a shot at that again. You understand, right?"

Jobe gave him the semblance of a smile. "Of course I get it. I wish you nothing but the best." He clapped Ray on shoulder in friendship.

The two knew the path through the cemetery to the best spot to hop a train. They had walked it in the dark many times; this time though they were being watched. Old Dawg slipped around in the bushes, trying to be quiet and avoid their attention. He was a tree trunk of a man. Tall and broad shouldered, strong but weak all at the same time. He was territorial as hell and everyone in Erwin and everyone passing through knew it, too. He had been listening and had heard Jobe's threat. He would beat the skinny piece of shit down for good—and this time, he would do it himself.

Ray and Jobe had stopped in a little bend in the rails, which most of the hoboes called it the "gettin on place." The curve provided privacy from the bulls and broke the line of sight for anyone on the ground to see a hobo jumping on a freight car. It was not easy business getting up on a slow moving train; it took lots of practice and even more luck.

"I guess, I'll see you around," said Jobe as he and Ray shook hands. "Good luck with everything."

"Don't be a stranger; careful out there!" Ray waved, stepped away, and walked back down the tracks towards the wall that led up behind the YMCA.

Jobe shuffled his feet as he stood in the shadows waiting for his ride. He had heard the whistle blow and knew it wouldn't be long. He rubbed at the knot on the back of his head as he puffed on a *cigarette.*

"Damn that bull and Dawg, too!" he said to himself.

"What was that? Damn me did you?" Old Dawg stepped out of the bushes across the tracks from Jobe.

The men squared their shoulders, only a set of train tracks separating them. Anger gleamed in Jobes' eyes, but hatred blackened Old Dawg's heart, filling him until it reached his eyes. Truth be told Jobe wasn't going to be much of a match for Old Dawg, who must have outweighed Jobe by a good fifty or sixty pounds. It wasn't going to be much of a fight anyway; the rumble of the engine and the train behind it was fast approaching. They could feel it in the ground, the tracks, even in their bones.

"Tell me something," said Jobe. "What did I do t' make you hate me so much?"

"Ha!" guffawed Old Dawg. "What makes you think you had do something? Ain't you heard? I am worse than the devil himself." He laughed again as if it was some big joke.

"You know," said Jobe, trying to keep his cool, "next time I am around this way, I think I will have a chat with the sheriff, not the railroad bulls you have in your pocket. After that I may catch a south bound out to Lost Cove and have a chat with your momma. I bet she don't have a clue what you been doing to people and she could still yank a knot in your tail no matter what size you are."

Jobe had played his last card. He had stopped around in Lost Cove about a year or two ago and stayed a few days. He had met this one lady, Cora; she had been right unpleasant at first but Jobe had a way with people. His genuine kindness tended to cause people to open up to him. She had spoken of her son who hadn't visited her in years and she figured he was dead and gone.

"It is Leonard, right?" asked Jobe. "Cora has your pleasant demeanor, but she was nice enough. You ought to go see your momma. I would go see mine if I could."

Old Dawg paled in the moonlight. "How did you——?" He was so stunned he couldn't finish.

"So, Leonard it is," said Jobe. "She described you as being just like your daddy. Showed me an old family picture. You look just like him." Jobe was raising his voice to get the last bit in; the train would round the corner any minute, and he would hop on and be gone before Old Dawg even knew Jobe had escaped.

The light from the engine was carving through the night, nearly blinding them both. Jobe tipped his hat, smiled, and flicked his cigarette butt towards Old Dawg, "See you next time. Leonard."

The train in all its glory was only a few feet away from them when Old Dawg launched himself at Jobe. They both fell to the one side of the track, just far away enough to keep them from being pulled under the mallet's gigantic wheels.

Dawg landed a punch and then another as Jobe pulled his arms in front of his face to block. He brought his leg up and kneed Dawg in the back. It was distraction enough to land a solid punch to Dawg's chin, throwing him back so Jobe scrambled out from under him. Jobe pushed himself to his feet, his head pounding even harder than it had been to when he came to earlier. The train was beginning to pick up speed; if he meant to be on it, northbound, he'd better jump on now.

Jobe ran towards the train, waiting for a freight car and maybe some help if others had already made it up. He knew Dawg would follow him, so he kept glancing over his shoulder and saw that Dawg was catching up to him. Dawg had sped up and launched *himself again at Jobe to keep him from making it onto the train. Jobe dodged on instinct but Dawg caught his arm, knocking both of them off kilter. Dawg screamed in fear, pain, and rage as he was pulled under the train. Blood splayed across the bushes and the screaming was silenced and the eerie* thunk thunk *of the mallet's wheels didn't pause for the death. His body minus a few limbs was dragged to nearly Fishery before the crew knew something had happened.*

Jobe heard the screams but only for a second as he hit the bottom edge of the first freight car, and the impact threw him backwards from the train. His neck snapped back with such force there was no way anyone could survive it. He fell to the side of the tracks, and some of the men jumped off to help him. He was dead when they got to him, a cracked skull and a broken neck.

When the officials came to assess and clean up, one of them asked, "Who was it?" He didn't even bother to examine the body.

"Well, Old Dawg was dragged we think," said one of the men, clearly still shaken. "But Jobe here, we think he broke his neck and banged his head around a lot." At the name, the rail officer finally snapped to attention.

"Did you say Jobe?" he asked. He pulled back the sheet covering the body and shined a light over the man's face. "It can't be," he gasped. "His father is going to be beside himself."

"Sir," asked one of the hoboes who stayed to help Jobe, "you know this feller?"

"Don't you?" the officer asked, shocked that no one else knew the real identity of the man.

"We all called him Jobe." The man went on, "I reckon that was all we knew him by. Names don't mean the same when you live

like we do."

The stiff-necked officer just nodded and patted the upset man on the shoulder. "We will see that he is properly taken care of. You men were friends of his; I will overlook seeing you here tonight."

"You gonna tell us who that is?" asked the drifter.

"Jobe wanted to remain anonymous—I will leave it that way," answered the officer. "Besides, can't let his family name get caught up in all this here scandal." He turned to walk away. "Hell, once his daddy breezes into town, they may name the damn cemetery after him."

"What about the other feller?" the drifter yelled after the officer.

"What other feller?" replied the officer. "Sometimes it is best to let sleeping dogs lie." He tipped his hat and walked off into the early light of dawn.

• •

The images faded with the puff of Jobe's cigarette. Aliza gaped at the gruesome and difficult memory she had just witnessed. She was quiet for a little while and sat down on the edge of the rail, realizing how she sometimes didn't consider other people's troubles because she was caught up in her own.

"So, Leo hates you because you found out about his family?" she questioned, carefully.

"After that first run I made with Ray where I met Cora, I went home to talk to my old man. But there was something else. She showed me a picture of her boy's daddy. Leo looked just like him. I don't." He waited for the words to sink in.

"Wait," she stopped and looked at him, "you and that brute are brothers?"

"Half," said Jobe. "Half-brothers. Apparently my dad went a little wild right before he and my mom married. He found out his previous girlfriend was pregnant and to keep her from telling Mom, he sent her to live in Lost Cove. Leo is maybe a year older than me. I don't think he even knew we were brothers, but we sure as hell fought like we were. I confronted my dad and he denied it. I told him I knew for sure. He threatened to cut me out of the will if I didn't drop it, so I did him one better. I left again. This time for good. I didn't need his money or his approval."

"What about Leo?" she asked. "Did you ever tell him?"

"I never really got the opportunity," said Jobe. "I asked around about him when I got back into Erwin, and he took it as a threat. He wasn't a very nice guy, so many hobos were afraid of him. Legend credits him with killing several people and I tend to believe it. I mean I was one of them, but I wonder if it would have been different if he had just listened."

"Isn't that the truth?" agreed Aliza. "If my brothers or my family listened just a quarter of the time I think I would feel less invisible. I have thoughts and dreams and just because I am a girl it seems like they don't care."

"Keep at it, Little Lady," he smiled. "They are bound

to hear you eventually."

"So, what's with Leo trying to get me to kill my brothers? Is that oddly directed at you?"

"I think Leo is just compelled to be evil, like he was when he was alive. He can't physically touch the knife because it is legendary for how he killed most of the people, but he can convince others to do it for him. It feeds his need to kill and be evil," said Jobe, matter-of-factly.

"But you are allowed to smoke?" she asked, skepticism edging her voice.

"Well, it was a concession for the job that I do," he said, lighting a new cig on the old one as it died out.

"What does that mean?"

"Well, it is a special something allowed to me as a ghost for putting up with Leo's shit and protecting people who come looking for trouble from him. I am also a bit of a tour guide," he said, gazing off into the dark.

"A tour guide and your brother's keeper," she chuckled, "and all you get is to smoke? Sounds down right lousy."

"It gives me just enough of a sensation of what it was like to be alive that I don't mind that it's all," he shrugged.

"Now explain the tour guide thing," she all but demanded.

"Well, I am a Wayward," he said, like she knew what it would be. Her looked told him she did not. "A Wayward is a ghost who was killed while traveling and therefore was offered the opportunity to help those who have," he hesitated, "lost their way. It fit for me because I lost my way a few times in life, too."

"So you like scare runaways?" she asked simply.

"Sometimes just seeing a ghost scares them and they run home," he admitted. "I think you are the first solid conversation I have had since this became my job."

"So, you think I should just go home? I don't think anything is going to change. Why the hell would I go back there?" she questioned. "You left because you knew your dad wasn't going to change, so what is the difference?" Her voice was getting louder. "Everything changed when Mason didn't come back! Everything. My parents always covering up their sadness with pointless talk. My brothers are either being jackasses or so caught up in their own shit that they can't do anything but play pranks on me. I really doubt they will miss me. Maybe I want to feel the wind in my hair and be gone, too." Her voice was raw with grief, bitterness, and pain.

Jobe gave her some space as she began to cry. He eventually rejoined her. As he sat down next to her, he said, "Ever say that to them?"

"No!" she spouted. "They wouldn't listen."

Jobe knew his job was getting harder by the moment. "Can I tell you the first thing I remember after becoming a ghost?"

"Whatever," she shrugged, wiping tears from her face.

"After I became a Wayward, the first place they put me was the cemetery. My daddy was standing at my grave, stern-faced as ever. He finally spoke. At first I thought it was to me, but I realized he couldn't see me.

But he addressed me. 'Jobe, I am sorry son. I should have listened to you and done right. When they told me what happened, I—I—well, I don't even have the words to explain. I bought the cemetery and named it after you. I am going to look for Leonard. I went to see his mother. You were right son.' He looked up and I swear he was looking at me, but I knew he couldn't see me. I think he started to cry, but the rain hid his tears."

She sniffled after a long silence. "So, what are you saying?"

"I saw what mine and even Leo's death did to my father," started Jobe. "He did search all over the area for Leo but never really found out anything because he was buried where they found his body, not in this cemetery."

"But I am not dead," snapped Aliza. "Uhh, sorry, I mean no offense."

"I know that, but my father lost two sons in one horrific event. Your family seems to have already lost one child. If they lose two, what will that do to them?"

Aliza chewed on the idea for a few minutes. Her mom and dad would speak even less and probably stop caring about each other. Her brothers would move away and never visit. But, what about her? Would it really work to go home and talk until they finally had to listen?

"How do you know it will work, if I go home?" asked Aliza.

"I don't," said Jobe plainly. "But you will have to live with 'what if' for the rest of your life. Are you going to do that with your family or without them?"

"Will you—" Aliza hesitated. "Will you help me?"

"I thought that was what I was doing already," said Jobe as he motioned for her to stand.

"We should probably head back to Erwin," she said. "I bet we have walked for miles."

As they ambled back, there was a low rumble recognized as a train. It was headed towards Erwin.

"Want to ride the rails a little?" Jobe smiled mischievously.

"I can't jump on a moving train!" blurted Aliza. "Are you crazy?"

"I can help." Jobe reached out and touched her arm, and in a bluish flash they were on the train car.

"Wow! How did you—?" She didn't finish as she was mesmerized by the rocking of the train, the wind on her face, and the seemingly billions of stars that winked at her.

When they got back to the cemetery they exited the train much the same way they boarded. Jobe helped her plan a way to get her family to listen and was maybe recruited to help with a prank or two against her brothers. They arrived at the back of Jobe Cemetery just as the first light shown in the sky. She could make out the forms of her two brothers passed out on the porch, exhausted from a night of searching the cemetery and being terrified of Old Dawg.

"Thank you," said Aliza, looking at the bluish form of Jobe as he changed to almost normal coloring in the brightening light of the dawn. "I would hug you if I could. I mean, it figures someone finally listens to me and he happens to be a ghost." She chuckled.

"Well, we do hear a lot more than you would think," he smiled. "I'll be around."

"And don't forget what I told you to do to them brothers."

• • •

EPILOGUE

Aliza strolled through the dewy morning grass of the cemetery and found the old rusty knife and her baseball bat only a few steps away. She stepped over the knife and picked up the bat. She walked the rest of the way to the house. Ian and Jack had passed out on opposite ends of the porch swing. She dropped the wooden bat so it would hit the swing and clank loudly on the porch. The jolt woke her brothers and both of them screamed. It was moments before they were arguing with her about what the hell happened in the cemetery.

"Why don't you both shut up," she said. "I think Mom and Dad would find this story quite interesting."

"Indeed they would," said Helen as she finished opening the front door.

As they sat down at the dining room table, Aliza spun her story—well, parts of it. She did mention the term Wayward, which caused her mom to raise an eyebrow, and the names Old Dawg and Jobe, which peaked her Dad's interest. Since she had their attention, she brought up her oldest brother Mason and the room began to shut down.

"No!" she said. "You can't just shut down because he is MIA. We are still a family, and if we don't listen and try, it is going to tear us apart. I was wrong when I ran away but you were wrong too! You were wrong to not let me dream about my own possibilities. Times are changing and I need to be a part of that. I deserve to get to do the things that they do or the things that Mason—" she choked up on his name.

"You are so totally right Aliza," said a voice that had not previously been a part of the conversation. "I let myself in."

They turned to see Mason standing in the doorway in his uniform. He was a lot thinner and looked like a shadow of himself, but he had the same gleam in his eye he always did.

Aliza got to him first and hugged him so tight that she thought for a moment she might break him. Everyone began their questions and Aliza gave up the spotlight. But she had a feeling that they would listen more and try harder, especially Jack and Ian after she told them that she told Old Dawg their names.

After the excitement of Mason's and Aliza's return,

she was sitting on the porch with her mother one evening. Jobe's form appeared at the edge of the cemetery and a familiar puff of smoke suggested he knew everything was all right.

AMY N. EDWARDS was born and raised in Unicoi, Tennessee. She attended East Tennessee State University and earned a bachelor's degree in English and a master's degree in administration. She teaches English and creative writing at her alma mater, Unicoi County High School, and comes home every day to her spoiled-rotten, sassy dog Jasper. Her debut novel *Seeker of the Rose*, published in 2011, was inspired by her European travels. She continues to work on numerous writing projects—and she's still addicted to travel.

ACKNOWLEDGMENTS

BEKAH HARRIS

Publishing a work of fiction, no matter the scope, takes the dedication and hard work of so many people. Thank you to Dustin Street for believing in my work and encouraging me to contribute to this project. Without him, I might never have taken the time to write about a haunted mansion that has intrigued me since childhood. I am so passionate about celebrating the rich culture of Appalachia, and this project has given me the opportunity to share a piece of my heritage with the world. I am also thankful for the other talented authors who contributed to this anthology. Finally, I want to express my unfailing gratitude to my family. They have always viewed my writing projects as my calling and my passion, rather than a silly hobby, and I am grateful for their support and help as I continue to pursue my dreams.

TRACY SUE NEEDHAM

There are so many people who walked with me on this journey that it is hard to find the words to thank you all—know I love you each and every one. My heart is full of gratitude. For David, my best friend and my rock; to Selena, my Dreamweaver whose light illuminated the way; for Nate, Joe, and the #ThingADay project, thank you for rekindling my love of words; to Judy, my beta reader and sounding board; for Haylee, the bright light in my life; to Mike for all your encouragement and belief in me; the Scranton Wrimos for all their support; and for Cassie and Luna, whose talks are greatly missed, I wish you were both here to see this.

J. WARREN WELCH

I would like thank Dustin Street and all of the other amazing authors who have come together on this exciting project.

ACKNOWLEDGMENTS (CONT)

S.S. MARSHALL

Throughout my life, I have been blessed with continued outpourings of love and support. I want to, without hesitation, thank my family and circle of friends for always backing me and my dreams. My daddy, for always holding my hand and helping me to grow in so many ways. My best friend Kelley, for believing in me and pushing me through this thing called life. And to the memory of my Mama, Allie Marshall; everything I do is for you. I hope I am making you proud.

DUSTIN STREET

It's hard to know where to begin on this one. This book has been two long years in the making, and I couldn't be prouder of how it turned out. I first have to thank the seven other authors who helped bring this collection of tales to life. I'm especially grateful to Amy N. Edwards—my one and only "Al"—for being a longtime friend, fellow writer, and confidante. This is the third anthology in which our work has appeared together, and I'm looking forward to many more writing adventures—plus many future opportunities for us to play "Acknowledgments Tag." To Aimee Renee, who took the reins on this project with vigor and excitement and edited this anthology to its pristine final product, I cannot thank you enough. You are a superstar who went above and beyond, and I look forward to having you on the BSTB team moving forward. To my aunt, Dee Dee Mitchell, who inspired me to write Kate's story in the first place, thank you for giving my imagination a jumping-off point! I dedicate my story, "Light," to my late grandfather, Cecil Barnett, whom the Light followed home many years ago—though I should hope under much less dire circumstances. And finally, to our readers who support us by consuming our stories, thank you so much! Without you, we'd just be sending our words out into the void.

ACKNOWLEDGMENTS (CONT)

DENVER MUNCEY

I would like to thank my family and friends for supporting me throughout this process. Most importantly, I would like to thank my late grandfather, Larry Torbett. You instilled a creativity and passion in me that I will treasure forever.

PATRICK BRIAN COOLEY

The list is long—from teachers, professors, family and friends to mortal enemies and that one hateful Barista—each has shaped and inspired me in their own ways. None, however, deserve recognition by name more than my mother, for her unwavering, lifelong support. Thanks, Mom!

AMY N. EDWARDS

As always, love to my mom, Marsha Edwards, for all of the encouragement, proofreading, and hugs! I hope you enjoy the memories. Thank you Drew Howell for talking ideas with me and helping Aliza and Jobe step out of the cemetery! I appreciate Debbie Bennett for reading and giving me some feedback! Big hugs to my dear friend, fellow writer, and Grammar Guru, Dustin Street. (Remember, only you can call me AL!) I thank God for the joy in words and writing!

Made in the USA
Coppell, TX
26 April 2020

22640642R00148